THIRST

THIRST

BY PETE LARSON

BLEAK HOUSE BOOKS

MADISON | WISCONSIN

Published by Bleak House Books
a division of Big Earth Publishing
923 Williamson St.
Madison, WI 53703
www.bleakhousebooks.com

ISBN 13 (cloth): 978-1-932557-40-4

Library of Congress Cataloging-in-Publication Data has been applied for.

Printed in the United States of America

11 10 09 08 07   1 2 3 4 5 6 7 8 9 10

For Julie, whom I fell in love with ten years after I wrote this book and who made it better.

Chapter ★ One

My customers were thirsty. A slab of high pressure had parked over Texas, leaving throats dry, tempers short, and three dead from "heat related causes." The air conditioner in the Longhorn Lounge struggled overtime to keep folks cool and friendly. I did what I could, pouring beer, listening here, talking there, keeping the wheels on the rails.

It seemed to be working. No drunks, no fights, no problems. The usual Thursday crowd gathered for the Sundown Boys. The Boys had kicked into an old Bob Wills number—"I miss you darlin', more and more every day"—when she sat down at the bar.

Pauline, our waitress, called from the middle of the bar, "Four frozen, Stu boy, one no salt."

"Be right with you," I told the woman. I blended the margaritas for Pauline, then put a napkin on the bar in front of the woman. She was tall and slim, with shoulder-length, brown hair and the kind of good looks that make you feel like you're an extra in her movie. She wore blue jeans and a white linen shirt. Her right eye caught the red neon glow of the Lone Star beer sign. A glass eye.

Nothing unusual about a woman coming into the Longhorn alone. Brownie, the owner, has been known to wield a baseball bat when a male customer gets disrespectful. I pegged the woman for white wine. She ordered bourbon, on the rocks, no water.

I poured the drink and set the glass on the bar. While she looked back at the band, I studied the right side of her face. Prominent cheekbone, pouty lips, dark, almost black eyebrow. A faint, thin scar sprouting upward like a single blade of grass from the corner of her eye.

The Boys finished their song and she turned her good eye in my direction.

"An accident," she said.

"Excuse me?" I pretended I didn't know she knew I'd been staring at her face. I picked up a bar rag and rubbed a non-existent spill.

"My mother hit me in the face with a golf club when I was five. An accident. I wandered into her backswing. Her first words were, 'Can't you watch where you're going?'"

She swallowed some whiskey. "People usually want to know. I thought I'd save you the trouble."

"Thanks."

"My turn. How long have you been bald?"

"Since I was fifteen. One day my hair started falling out; six months later I was Mr. Clean."

"Bend down."

I leaned over the bar. She stood up and reached for my head, trailing her fingers over the bare skin. I hadn't been touched like that in a long, long time. The softball players at the end of the bar started hooting. She acted as if they didn't exist.

"Smooth."

"Don't give the boy too much attention." Pauline leaned in next to the woman. "His head's way big enough as is."

The woman laughed and the Sundown Boys slid into "San Antone Rose."

She stayed at the bar for the rest of the set. We talked a bit between songs, about weather, the music. Mostly I poured drinks and washed glasses. I looked at her whenever I could, drawn as much as anything to the flaws, the false eye, the pale scar.

One time she stared back at me. I turned away first. Another time she glanced quickly away and spoke with Pauline.

The next time I looked, her stool was empty, her glass on the back edge of the bar to make it easier to clean up. Sometimes a little unexpected attention is all it takes to keep the planet in orbit.

Sometimes not. Three hours later, after locking up the bar, I pulled my pickup truck into the alley behind Jack's Hardware. She sat at the top of the wooden stairs leading up to my apartment, her face in deep shadows from the 60-watt bulb over the door.

"Your waitress friend told me where you live," she said as I started up the stairs. "If you want me to leave, just say the word."

"I don't have an air conditioner. Just a fan."

"I like fans."

I unlocked the door.

I woke. Motes of dust slow danced in the morning sun above the empty pillow at my side.

I sat up, naked on the sweaty sheets, and closed my eyes, recalling how we silently undressed each other, how she lifted her arms overhead as I traced the long line of her body with my fingers, and how she watched my face as she returned the favor. We fell into each other like two people who discover they're hungry only after they start eating. I didn't know which I wanted more, to touch or be touched, and I wasn't alone in my longing.

Since the break-up of my marriage two years earlier, I'd had only one, unfortunate fling with an old college friend who felt sorry for me, twice. Before that, increasingly perfunctory lovemaking with Jocelyn, my ex-wife. We were married for five years. For at least half that time, Jocelyn found physical contact with me a chore. Maybe I did, too.

I opened my eyes and stared at the patch of sunlight on the far wall as I struggled with a growing unease. The night before, it had seemed like a fine idea; two consenting adults giving each other some much needed comfort. But in the morning that sounded more like an excuse.

I had no idea who she was. If I had, things might have turned out differently.

Chapter ★ Two

On Friday nights we hold an open mike at the Longhorn. Charlie and Nelda, a brother and sister duo in matching, purple Western shirts, opened with one of their own, "You're the Rock of My Gibraltar." I worked my way along the bar, mostly drafts and bottles. Louise, a taxi dispatcher with a voice like rock candy, passed around pictures of Paws, a tabby kitten abandoned in the back seat of a cab. Zach, from the English Department at the university, reported a clear GI series. I slipped him a bourbon and soda on the house.

I spotted John Springer as I taped a snapshot of Paws to the side of the cash register.

"Stuart. Good to see you. How have you been doing?"

"Fine, John. You slumming tonight?" I pointed to his clerical collar and set a glass of Johnny Walker Black in front of him. With his finely trimmed beard and expertly combed hair he looked more like an advertisement for Rogaine than the senior pastor of one of the largest churches in the city.

John laughed and rested his hand on my forearm. In seminary we called it the *touch touch*. John's one of the few ties to my old life that I haven't been able to sever. I looked at his hand. He even grooms his fingernails. I pulled away my arm.

"I dressed up for the mayor," he said. "Nothing important." He held up the bourbon in a silent toast and took a small sip. "I assume she's been in touch."

"Who's been in touch?"

John stroked the brown whiskers on his chin.

"You mean she hasn't called you? My, my."

"John, what the hell are you talking about?"

"I hate to be the one to tell you this, Stuart. The Reverend Jocelyn Wendell Graham has accepted the position of assistant minister at Community Congregational Church."

Jocelyn? Here in Travis City? It didn't make sense. I felt queasy, like seeing a pillar of smoke across town where your apartment should be.

"Is this some kind of joke?"

"She called earlier in the week. I naturally assumed she'd informed you."

"You're serious. She's moving here?"

"More likely already moved. I understand they're installing her on Sunday."

"Why did she contact you?"

"Professional courtesy, Christian fellowship, networking with an old seminary classmate. You know the routine."

I ignored the jab and went off to fill an order. Jocelyn. Here. Now. I'd always figured I'd run into her again some day. I just hadn't expected to share a town with her again. Damn her. She at least owed me a warning.

John sat on his stool, sipping his drink and watching me. I stopped in front of him

"If you're waiting to extend some pastoral care," I said, "forget it. I couldn't care less about the Reverend Graham."

"Actually, I have a favor to ask. I'm taking a church group to Honduras for two weeks in August. I hope you'll fill in for me the first Sunday."

"You know I don't preach anymore." I spoke louder than I meant to.

He handed me a five-dollar bill. "You don't have to let me know now. Think about it." He winked and walked out.

Asshole.

I filled the sink with scalding water and began scrubbing glasses, but I couldn't rub off the news of Jocelyn's arrival. Or the feeling that John Springer was pressing my buttons like I was the Wurlitzer at Rangers Stadium.

"Stu. Two more Shiners." Chris Stark, an artist who stopped at the Longhorn three or four nights a week, held out two empties. He looked like a black velvet painting by Jackson Pollock, black T-shirt and jeans dribbled with lines of red, green, and blue. Daniel Lackland, who shared a studio with Chris and sat on the next stool, looked more like an Andrew Wyeth portrait of a none too successful accountant: short, brown hair over a round, boyish face, and a forest of pencils and pens in his breast pocket.

I grabbed the empties from Chris and opened three Shiners. I handed one to Chris and passed him a

Tabasco bottle. He shook a few drops into his beer. To each his own.

I set the second beer in front of Daniel, who was making small, steady movements with a felt tip pen over the back of a bar coaster.

"Can I see it?"

He looked up and blushed, as if I'd caught him swigging from the milk carton.

"It's nothing. You know. Just a sketch," he said as he slid his work across the bar. The coaster held a likeness of Rusty Martin, my fellow bartender, filling a pitcher at the tap, the details of Rusty's hands and the foaming liquid rendered in tiny, precise lines, yet with an overall impression of movement and energy.

"I like the flow of beer," I said, handing him back the drawing. "Those four little lines."

"It's the light. On the beer, I mean. The way the light looks on the beer."

"Can I give it to Rusty when you're finished?"

"Sure. I guess. If you want." He was head down again, scribbling on the coaster.

I took a long step to the right end of the bar, sliding the third bottle of Shiner to Harry Clintock on the last stool.

"God Bless the Child," he rumbled as he engulfed the bottle with a hand the size of a catcher's mitt. Harry's our unofficial bouncer. He talks in song titles and fragments, mostly top forty from the Sixties and early Seventies. He's spent the last twenty years in and out of VA hospitals.

"You Can't Always Get What You Want," I said.

A hand tapped my forearm.

"Another pitcher of sangria, Bar Keep."

I'd never been called "Bar Keep" before. Usually it's Bud, Mac, Big Guy, or Chrome Dome. When I turned I expected to see a tweedy sort, like David Niven in *Around the World in Eighty Days*. Instead I saw a little urban cowboy in a suede jacket, a string tie with a silver and turquoise clasp, and a silver lizard pin on his lapel. He had traditional good looks, square face, square jaw, straight ahead gray eyes. A tiny ponytail of unnaturally black hair stuck out from the back of his head like a fuse.

"How many glasses?"

"We're all set, my friend." He gestured vaguely behind him and gave me the sort of you're-a-special-fellow smile that you can't help responding to, even if you don't quite believe it.

I nodded, pulled a pitcher from under the bar, filled it halfway with ice, and turned for the vat of sangria on the back bar.

I inspected the stranger in the mirror as he leaned between Chris and Daniel. They didn't share my interest. Chris smiled grimly and toyed with a loose strand of his long, blond hair. Daniel huddled over his bar coaster.

The stranger looked to each side, then stepped back, putting his hands on their shoulders.

"Christopher, Daniel. I didn't recognize you from the back. How are you fellows doing?"

"Dr. Washburn," Chris replied. Daniel kept silent, as if the little cowboy wasn't there.

"Oh please, call me Andrew. Remind me when you finished."

"Three years ago."

"Three years." The stranger shook his head. "I've

heard fine reports about both of you. I understand you have paintings in the ArtFest exhibition. Congratulations."

Chris lifted his bottle slightly without looking up. There was history here. I shut off the spigot and busied myself garnishing the pitcher with orange slices and cherries, hoping I'd catch what was said.

"You know," the stranger continued, "it's always an honor when our graduates are selected for a juried exhibition. Are you still doing large color fields, or is it something new?"

Chris, his jaw muscles tight, scraped at the label on his bottle. Washburn regarded him for a moment, then turned toward Daniel.

"And I assume you've submitted one of those nice little landscapes."

A stool crashed to the floor. Daniel stood trembling, inches from the stranger. The music stopped and Harry moved in like a massive St. Peter: bushy, gray beard, eyes burning. I held up a hand to keep him back.

"Some day," Daniel stammered, his voice filling the room. "You'll get yours. Some day. I mean it." He shoved his way to the door.

After a pause, the crowd lost interest and the buzz of voices rose. I nodded to Charlie and Nelda to start playing. The stranger stooped to pick up the stool. He looked toward the door, then at Chris, then me, shrugging. I set the pitcher of sangria in front of him.

"I hope nothing's wrong with Daniel," he said to Chris. "Wish him luck at the exhibition. And of course the same to you."

He handed me a twenty. "I apologize for Daniel's

behavior. Use the change for his tab and Christopher's, and keep the rest for yourself." He gave me another of those smiles, then picked up the pitcher and excused his way through the crowd.

★

I cashed out the bill and opened another Shiner.

I set the cold beer in front of Chris. "Seems to be paid for," I said. "Who was that? I didn't know Daniel could get that angry."

"Andrew Washburn. Dean of Fine Arts and Mayor of Weaselville." Chris looked to each side, then hunched forward over his beer bottle, the nostrils on his thin nose flaring as he spoke. "Fucking son of a bitch won't get off Daniel's ass." He leaned back. "You don't know about Washburn, do you?"

"Never saw him before tonight."

"Daniel's wife ditched him for Washburn. Couple of years ago. Leaves a note on the bed. No fight, no warning, nothing. She's been at it with Washburn all along, I figure. She gets the divorce, marries Washburn the next day. Wham, bam. Daniel goes Clam City. Never talks about it."

I stared at the blue glow of the jukebox, back in my own marriage again. A couple of years ago, same as Daniel's. Kablooie. The earth opened. That's the way it is when your wife picks up with another man. It swallowed my home, my future, most of what I thought was me. I lost my calling, left the church. Driving without headlights in those days, nothing to lose. So much for forgetting Jocelyn. I looked at Chris.

"This guy's been taunting Daniel?"

"Beaucoup. We're at a party last winter. In walk Washburn and Gwen—that's Daniel's ex. Daniel tries to split. Washburn nails him. Says he's heard so much about Daniel from Gwen. Wants to get to know him. Invites him to dinner." Chris took a long drink. "Fucking bastard."

"What did she do?"

"Gwen? Looked like she wanted to hang Washburn by his frigging ponytail. I think she's still got a soft spot for Daniel. She fucked him over, but I don't know. . ." Chris shrugged and turned to watch three guys in Hawaiian shirts set up to play next.

I pulled a couple of drafts and studied Washburn. He held forth at a table in front of the bandstand. I told myself that if C.J. Walker Jr. ever taunted me in public about sleeping with Jocelyn, I'd just slice him with a few well-honed remarks. Jocelyn's the one to blame. C.J. just hitched a ride.

Chris declined when I held up another beer.

"I've been pretty close to the edge myself," I mused. "You do things you regret."

"You think Daniel will do something wacko?"

"Two years is a long time," I said. "He's not crazy."

"I hope not." Chris handed me the coaster from in front of Daniel's stool. The delicate drawing had been scratched through with hard, quick strokes that tore into the cardboard. "I better check on him."

"Good idea," I said. "I'm tending bar at the ArtFest Reception. You two be there?"

"Count on it."

As Chris walked out, I buried the coaster in the trash

can. I wanted to believe Daniel wouldn't do anything crazy two years after the fact, any more than I would.

Four hours later, I saluted the empty bar and upended my ritual glass of single malt scotch whiskey, letting the last drops of Highland Park roll across my tongue and trace a warm trail down my throat. I put the glass in the sink, switched off the lights, and made my way down the back hallway by the red glow of the exit sign.

I smelled Bob the Prophet in the alley as I leaned against the metal door, closing the padlock. The first scent was sweet wine; the second, old, old sweat, the kind that comes from a gym locker that never got cleaned out over the summer.

"Bob? It's Stu. I'm locking up. Have a good one."

His loud voice sounded from behind the dumpster.

"The Hand Tools of God are coming." *Boom.* He slammed a fist against the steel container. "Coming for you."

Normally I leave Bob to his omens and portents. But that night I stopped.

"Why are the Hand Tools coming, Bob?"

Boom, boom. "The Hand Tools of God are coming." *Boom.* "Coming to fix you."

"Why do I need fixing?"

"The Wrench of the Baptist." *Boom.* "The Hammer of the Lamb." *Boom, boom.*

Bob carried on booming and I headed home.

I could have roasted chestnuts in my apartment. I

propped the door open with a brick and positioned a
sinking, overstuffed chair in the faint cross breeze, then
took two steps to the kitchen. I poured a beer into one of
the recycled peanut butter jars that constitute my glass-
ware and doled out the weekly water ration to my three
cacti, Shadrach, Meshach, and Abednego.

On my way back to the living room, I paused to look
at a napkin taped to the front of my refrigerator. It was a
drawing of Daniel Lackland's from a few weeks ago. He
sketched the back of my head and shirt as I stood at the
cash register. In the living room, I picked up the remote
and flipped through the channels. Nothing but *Dukes of
Hazard* reruns and infomercials for belly exercisers. I
clicked off and leafed through a stack of old *National
Geographic*s. Nothing held my attention. Out of
desperation I pulled *Moby Dick* from the bookcase. The
bookmark was at page ninety-one where I'd left it two
months ago. One paragraph into it I gave up. If I didn't
find something to do, I'd spend the next three hours reliv-
ing the death of my marriage.

A row of volumes—all hardbound in sober shades of
blue and brown—gazed at me from the top shelf. I don't
know why I kept them; I hadn't cracked a book of sermons
in the two years since I walked out on the church. In the
two years since walking in on Jocelyn and C.J.

I sipped the beer. A cold and welcome bitterness filled
my mouth. Why not? Jocelyn never appreciated a fine sermon, mine or anyone else's. I pulled down a collection of
Jonathan Edwards and opened to "Sinners in the Hands of
an Angry God."

"The wrath of God burns against them, their

damnation does not slumber; the pit is prepared, the fire is made ready, the furnace is now hot, ready to receive them; the flames now rage and glow."

If the Holy Hand Tools were coming, might as well stoke the furnace.

CHaPTeR ★ THRee

Coils of heat contorted the air above the blacktop as I
unloaded my pickup behind the Travis University Student
Center the following Sunday afternoon. I tried to recall the
physics of refrigeration. Something to do with the relation
between pressure and temperature. After I get paid for the
reception, I promised myself, I'd buy a new air conditioner.

I run my own bartending business out of the
Longhorn, mostly weddings and big parties. I buy the
booze at cost plus twenty percent from Brownie, and she
lets me keep my supplies in the storeroom. References
available upon request.

I'd hired Pauline to handle orders from tables, and
Steve Lewis, a geology grad student, to pour at a second
bar. We set up in the President's Rooms, which was actually one long, high-ceilinged room with beige wallpaper,
tan curtains, beige carpeting, and off-white ceiling tiles. A
space with no personality of its own, waiting for something to happen.

The reception started at five and filled up fast, a vintage gathering of Texas art and money. Tuxedos and designer dresses, cowboy hats and boots, torn T-shirts and slashed blue jeans. Blue hairs, long hairs, short hairs, purple hairs. By quarter to six we had a glass or bottle in the hands of most of the 250 guests.

I caught myself watching the doors, convinced that Jocelyn would appear, resenting the unavoidable fact that I cared. Daniel and Chris walked in. Daniel wore a short sleeve, white shirt, dark blue tie, and dark blue slacks. You have to love a guy whose idea of dressing up is to imitate a Mormon missionary. Chris had chosen the all white look: T-shirt, jacket, painter's pants, and sneakers. His hair, unfurled, dropped straight to his shoulders like a beardless California Jesus. I invited them behind the bar to chat.

"How you fellows doing?" I asked.

Daniel only shrugged and turned a beer bottle around in his hands. Chris jumped in. "Primo," he replied, his body in constant motion even when he stood still. I imagined this was their custom at parties: Chris' buzz providing protective cover for Daniel.

"When does the exhibition open?" I asked.

"Two weeks. I'll score you an invitation to the opening."

"Thanks. I'm looking forward to seeing your work."

"Shit, don't wait for the exhibition. Stop by the studio. Old Texas Sun canning factory, ground floor. Where Santa Clara hits the river. Okay with you, Daniel?"

Daniel blinked. "Sorry," he mumbled. "Sure, fine."

Pauline pulled up at the bar. She'd dressed up for the event, swapping her usual Willie Nelson T-shirt for a lime green bowling shirt with "Al" stitched over the pocket.

"Some of that fancy ass scotch on the rocks, two white wines, and a Lite."

"What kind of scotch?"

"Glen somebody or something. For the tightwad with the teeny ponytail. You know the one. He was in the Longhorn the other night. Cross between John Wayne and a used car salesman."

"He tipped me pretty good. Didn't he leave anything on the table?" I dropped two cubes in a highball glass and selected the bottle of Glenfiddich. I covered the ice with a shot from the triangular bottle. A sweet, woody smell rose from the amber liquid.

"Shit, honey, he didn't leave me enough to make a parking meter fart." As she shook her head in disgust, I marveled, as I always do, at Pauline's hair, a mass of red that billows endlessly up and out like cotton candy on steroids. Sometimes I wish she were single and ten years younger than forty-something.

I emptied a wine bottle into a glass, then discovered I didn't have any backups under the bar.

"I've got to run out to the hall and fetch a couple more whites," I told Pauline. "Hold down the fort." When I returned with the wine bottles, Pauline was chatting with a bald man wearing an "Art Attack" T-shirt. Daniel and Chris were talking with a young woman in an iridescent blue, Fifties prom dress.

"Order up," I called, after filling the glasses.

As Pauline carried away the tray of drinks, a woman entered through the main doors. A woman I knew. She had brown hair the color of Jocelyn's, but was taller and more elegant, wearing a blue silk blouse over a short, black leather skirt. She was as gorgeous as I remembered. She scanned the room, looking for someone with her one good eye.

Daniel bolted from the bar. The last I saw of him he almost ran through the crowd toward the back of the room.

"Is he okay?"

"Gwen just walked in," said Chris.

Gwen Washburn. Andrew Washburn's wife, Daniel's ex, and the stranger I slept with three nights ago. I felt myself flush as I fumbled with all the relationships, as if I'd just discovered that one plus one equals three. After I found Jocelyn in bed with another man, I took pride in the fact that I never committed adultery and never would, and that included sleeping with someone else who was married. The other night I had assumed Gwen wasn't married because she wasn't wearing a ring. But I didn't ask. I didn't even learn her name.

Gwen found her husband standing by a table in the middle of the room. If she spotted me she didn't show any sign of it.

"Daniel was married to her?" I asked Chris, suddenly feeling that I had stepped into the middle of someone else's hard story.

"Yeah. Well, she dresses up nice. I better go check on Daniel."

I changed positions to get a better view. The group of people around Washburn drifted away as Gwen approached. Only a young woman in a light blue dress remained by his side. A black band held long, blond hair out of her face. I could make out blue eyes, a smattering of freckles across her nose, and a line of white teeth. She froze when Gwen made a show of shaking her hand. Gwen turned toward Washburn, who kissed her on the cheek. He had to go up on tiptoes to reach her face. He put a proprietary arm around her waist; she pulled away. The chill from her voice reached across the room, though I couldn't make out the words.

Pauline tapped me on the head with her empty tray and then glanced over her shoulder in Gwen's direction. "Isn't that our friend from the other night? She find your place all right?"

"I didn't know she was married."

"My, my," said Pauline, taking a moment to put pieces together. "If that's a problem, sugar, you should have asked. I'll have a Dewar's on the rocks and a couple of Lone Stars."

I pulled out the beers, fighting down the urge to explain myself. By the time I'd filled the order, Gwen was moving away from Washburn and heading for the door. I looked in the direction Daniel had fled. Chris was already standing near the back doors. He shrugged.

I poured some white wine for a pair of Junior Leaguers and glanced over their heads. Washburn had gathered a new group of listeners. The young blond woman at his side glanced nervously toward the entrance.

Washburn picked his glass of scotch off the table and took a long drink. His eyes grew wide and he let out a loud, breathy cry. He stumbled backward, splashing the rest of the drink onto his chest. He fell, pitching to the side.

"Call an ambulance!" I shouted to Pauline, who was approaching the bar. I sprinted around the end and pushed through the crowd.

The guests in the ballroom began to realize that something had happened about the time I reached the table. The noise fell away in widening rings.

A small crowd was forming around Washburn, who lay on his side. His body convulsed every few seconds as if he were plugged into a socket of slowly alternating current. The young, blond woman knelt by him, her hand on his arm.

"Somebody do something!" she sobbed. "Please, somebody!"

I turned Washburn onto his back while someone moved her away. His eyes were closed and his features were locked in the exaggerated grimace of someone tasting sour milk. The convulsions weakened, yet remained strong enough to lift his feet off the floor. Shallow breathing going nowhere.

I looked up at Chris and Steve Lewis, my other bartender. "Hold him down."

Chris grabbed Washburn's wrists, while Steve held down his legs. I put a hand under Washburn's neck and tilted up his chin. I stuck two fingers into his mouth, opening up an air passage and making sure he hadn't swallowed his tongue. Then I pinched his nose and clamped my mouth over his, forcing my breath into his lungs. As I pulled back from his face, the smell of bitter almonds mixed with the smoky odor of scotch. The convulsions stopped.

I filled his lungs again, then ran my fingers along his neck. No pulse. The old training from high school YMCA class came into my head. Fifteen and two. Fifteen compressions, two ventilations. I positioned the heel of my hand on Washburn's chest and leaned over him, pushing down with straight arms.

"One and two and three and four . . ."

I locked into the rhythm of pressing his chest, blowing into his mouth, then back to the chest. Press. Press. Press. Blow. The world shrank down to the wet stain of scotch on Washburn's shirt, the scratchiness of his dry lips, the occasional clicking of our teeth, and the sickly, bitter scent of whiskey and almonds. Press. Press. Press. Blow.

A pair of strong hands gripped my shoulders and pulled me away. I looked up dizzily at two men in dark blue uniforms. One of them moved me into a chair while the other examined Washburn. He tore back Washburn's shirt, opened a blue metal case, and held up two paddles, thick metal pancakes leashed to the box by coiled cables. The other man uncapped a syringe, squirted a few drops into the air, and injected the contents into Washburn's chest. He took his hands away from the body and nodded. The first man placed the paddles on Washburn's chest. The torso jerked, as if Washburn were trying, for just a moment, to sit up. The second paramedic leaned over Washburn's face, then nodded to the other, who applied the paddles again and sent another fifty volts through his chest. Then a third time. A fourth.

"This is Unit 75," said the second paramedic into a walkie talkie. "We have a possible Code 3 on the university campus, in the student center, the President's Rooms."

"Roger," crackled the radio. "Assistance and CSU on the way."

He stowed the walkie talkie and came over to my chair. He had thick, black hairs on his forearms. I remember that. Black hairs like grass in the wind.

"You did good. There wasn't a blessed thing you coulda done. He was probably dead before you started CPR."

"Did he have a heart attack?" I asked, aware of my own heart pounding as if in someone else's chest. My shirt stuck to the drying sweat on my back.

"Heart attack? I doubt it. I might be wrong, but I'd say the man was poisoned."

The other paramedic pulled a sheet over Washburn. I looked down at the contour of head, arms, and legs under the sheet and pictured another body twenty years earlier — my mother's, wedged in a coffin too narrow for her broad shoulders, dressed in clothes I didn't recognize. It was her; but it wasn't. Something was missing, though at the time I couldn't say what. It didn't even seem like her body, as if someone had tried to make another dead person look like my mother. I suppose now I'd say her soul had left and taken her with it. At the time I just felt cheated.

The police had already set up shop, sealing the room and cordoning off the death site. A slow moving, scraggly line formed near the door, as an officer took down names and addresses before letting people go. Another cop corralled Chris and some other witnesses at a table at the back of the room. Two detectives, an older white guy and a younger Hispanic, questioned them one at a time. At a separate table, a female officer comforted the young woman who had stood next to Washburn. Pauline, Steve Lewis, and I (the hired help) were sequestered at yet another table. Daniel, of course, was gone. So was Gwen.

The paramedics removed the body on a wheeled stretcher. It seemed to float out of the room, steady and silent as a balloon. I had been there when he died, been right there, yet his body already seemed unreal to me. Pauline rubbed my shoulders and told me a story about the time her Aunt Arvell had to pull Uncle Patterson out from under a tractor. The sound of her voice wrapped around me like a great, wool blanket.

Chapter★Four

The police dismissed Steve after a brief conversation. The younger detective escorted Pauline to another table. The older one dropped a red, polyester sports coat onto the table where I sat. Cough-drop red. He had thin, greased-back hair and an ample gut covering most of a Dallas Cowboys belt buckle.

"Detective Drainer," he announced as he straddled the back of a chair and sat down. "You're the bartender who served the drink and the guy who tried to revive him, right?" he asked after taking my name and address.

I nodded.

"What was he drinking?" A toothpick wiggled up and down in a corner of his mouth.

"Glenfiddich. Scotch. In the triangular green bottle." The air-conditioning seemed to have cranked up. A chill locked onto my ribs. I hugged myself.

Drainer pulled out the toothpick and looked over at my bar, where men wearing blue overalls and latex gloves were loading the bottles into cardboard boxes.

"Careful with that three-sided green one. Bust that, it's your ass." He turned back to me, restoring the toothpick. "When's the last time anybody drank out of that bottle?"

"Last week. At the Longhorn Lounge over on Jarvis, where I work. I get my supplies there."

"D'you see anybody touch the drink other than you and the waitress?"

"No." I described how I had left the bar to get more wine after pouring the drink and before finishing the order.

"Where were you standing when he collapsed?"

"Behind the bar."

"How's it you got to the body first?"

"I didn't. I just started moving first."

"D'you know Dr. Washburn?"

"I knew he was the dean of Fine Arts."

"When's the last time you saw him, before tonight?"

"At the Longhorn. Thursday night. That was the first time I ever saw him."

Drainer wrote something in his notebook, his thick fingers dwarfing the ballpoint. "Any plans to leave town?"

"No."

"Good. Keep it that way."

"Was he poisoned?"

"No comment."

"But the paramedic said . . ."

"Paramedic's not the medical examiner." He stood up and pulled on his red sports coat. "When we're sure of the cause of death, we'll release it."

"What about my supplies?" I pointed to the empty bar.

"Evidence. You can get 'em back in a week, maybe two. Depends on what we find." The younger detective called from Washburn's table, where a technician inspected the surface under the purple glow of a handheld ultraviolet light. Drainer shoved the notebook into the inner pocket of his jacket and walked away.

I wandered over to the table that I had used as a bar. Without the white cloth it was merely a dented piece of one-inch plywood bolted to metal legs. Everything was gone—glasses, bottles, ice. I ran my fingers over the coarse surface and felt hot tears in my eyes. It's just a bunch of booze, I told myself. You're in shock. Get out of here.

I dried my eyes, then headed into the hallway, looking for Steve or Pauline. The only person there was a janitor buffing the floor. As I descended the marble stairs of the student center, I forced myself to do the math: $700 worth of booze, $150 for the glasses, another $200 for assorted supplies, shakers, strainers and ice chests. They even took the empties, so I had no idea how much to charge the reception committee. Normally I'd go back and demand my supplies or some cash to cover them. But I couldn't see my way to normal at the moment.

I climbed into the pickup. Heat from the vinyl seat spread through the back of my shirt and soaked into my skin. I closed my eyes and felt again the unresponsive bulk of Washburn's chest, the empty fleshiness of his lips. I'd been around corpses before. Hell, I'd been in the room when folks died. But I'd never come so close to touching death before. One moment he was a person and we were mouth to mouth. Then nothing, and I was blowing into a corpse.

People used to believe the soul leaves the body through the mouth, and if you watch closely, you can catch it slipping away. I didn't see a thing. I couldn't even tell when it happened.

The sun was still high when I reached my apartment. A line of shadow sliced the landing outside my door, my chest in light, my legs in darkness. I put the key in the lock, but then just stood there, my vision blurred, thinking of nothing, as if I was drifting with Washburn's body across a vast and vacant room.

"Enough," I said aloud, slapping the brick wall. "Go for a run."

I changed into shorts, T-shirt, and running shoes and pulled on a Milwaukee Brewers cap. I set out west on River Park Drive. Half a mile from my apartment the Drive crosses University and drops into River Park, on the old flood plain. The park hugs the west branch of the Brazos River. I cut across the softball fields to the bike path on the embankment. It had been dry since spring and the river was low. Twenty feet below me, the water was the color of muddy coffee and moving just as slow.

My cap was completely soaked by the one-mile mark and sweat filled my eyes. I hadn't run in a week. My lungs resisted the hot air. My legs begged to stop. It felt wonderful. I plodded through the swelter for another two miles, reassured by the earthly pain in my gut as I struggled back up the hill on River Park Drive.

The two police detectives were standing at the top of my stairs. Drainer's younger partner was a study in gray: pressed gray slacks, a gray and black tie, and a lightweight, gray jacket. He had a full head of black hair and a thick, black mustache. The corners of his mouth and the edges of his eyes seemed on the verge of a smile, as if he found his job pleasantly amusing.

"Sorry," I apologized, grabbing the railing to catch my breath. "I was running."

"Mr. Carlson, I'm Lieutenant Ramirez. We'd like to ask you a few questions. May we go in?"

"Sure." I mopped my face with a towel I'd left on the handrail. I pulled myself up the stairs and squeezed past Drainer. The landing wasn't built for three grown men. I unlocked the door and went in first.

"Sorry," I said, "no air-conditioning, but have a seat. I need some water. Can I get you anything?"

"No, thank you, Mr. Carlson."

I retreated to the kitchen. The police were actually trying to find out who killed Washburn. Drainer's questions earlier in the afternoon had been part of the fog I was moving through after trying to pound life into Washburn's chest. The death had seemed a fact of nature, something to be dealt with, not something to be solved. I downed a tumbler of water, then refilled the glass and tried to think clearly. If the paramedic was right, someone at the reception slipped a strong poison into Washburn's glass of scotch. Or someone managed to spike the bottle at my bar. Or poison the bottle even before it even left the Longhorn.

I'm one of the few people who drink from the single malts at the bar. If Washburn hadn't ordered Glenfiddich,

I might have taken the fatal drink and ended up writhing on the floor beside the beer cooler. I put my head under the running faucet to rinse off the salty crust of drying sweat. It didn't do a thing for the unwelcome thought.

When I returned to the main room, Ramirez was standing in front of my bookcase while Drainer slouched in one of the two overstuffed chairs. Ramirez turned, a copy of the Summa Theologica open in his hands. "You read Aquinas?" he asked in the tone a marathoner uses to inquire if you're a serious runner.

"I have. Not recently." The question startled me, as if he'd asked me to justify the way my life unfolded. He's just doing his job, I told myself, making me feel at ease so I'll answer the important questions later. He doesn't care about the fall of a small town minister.

He looked at me for a moment, then nodded. He returned the book to the shelf and sat down next to Drainer, who had shifted his chair to a position directly in front of the window fan.

"What can I do for you?" I asked as I pulled over a straight back chair. I avoided looking at the bookcase behind Ramirez. It wasn't just the sermons I'd kept. Most of the books were from my previous life, theology, biblical commentaries, church history. I hadn't decided to keep them; I just never decided to get rid of them.

"We would like to know some details of what happened at the ArtFest reception." Ramirez used the formal diction of a well-educated person who spoke English as a second language. It dawned on me that he, not Drainer, was in charge.

"When you were pouring the scotch," he continued, "did you know the drink was for Dr. Washburn?"

"Pauline—that's Pauline Rider, the waitress who was working with me—told me." I could hear the scrape of Ramirez's fountain pen on the notebook page above the hum of the fan.

"Does she always make a point of reporting for whom you are pouring drinks?"

"No. It's just that Dr. Washburn was in the Longhorn Lounge the other night. He gave me a good tip, but left her a lousy one."

"What night was that?"

"Thursday."

"Did you witness an exchange between Dr. Washburn and anyone else on Thursday night?" he asked.

The real purpose of the interview kicked me in the shin. The police thought Daniel poisoned Washburn. I rubbed my head to give myself time to think. I pictured Daniel standing in front of Washburn, blurting out, "You'll get yours." And now Washburn had. But it didn't make sense.

"Several witnesses reported that Daniel Lackland had a confrontation with Dr. Washburn that evening," Ramirez added. "Did you hear what Lackland said?"

Ramirez's use of Daniel's surname sounded juridical. Final. That clinched it for me. Ramirez had already decided Daniel was guilty. He didn't need my help and I wasn't going to offer it.

"It was loud, a busy night, and it was all I could do to hear people's orders."

Ramirez paused, regarding me with his gray, almost black eyes. I'm usually pretty good at bluffing in poker. But I wouldn't want to play against Ramirez. He knew I was telling less than the truth. And he knew that I knew he knew. None of which made me feel any more cooperative.

"Back to the reception," he continued. "Were there other people besides yourself who might have heard who the scotch was for?"

"There were a lot of people around the bar, talking, waiting for drinks. I really couldn't say . . ."

"Was there any way someone could have put something in the drink without your seeing it?"

"Like I told Detective Drainer, after I poured the scotch I ran out of wine and had to go out to the hall to get some more bottles. I was gone for a couple of minutes. Pauline was watching the bar for me."

"Was Lackland near the bar this whole time?"

"I have no idea."

"So he heard who the drink was for?"

"I was too busy pouring drinks to notice who was where." Fresh sweat rolled down my neck. My tiny apartment was hot enough without three grown men raising the temperature. Drainer mopped his face with a wadded handkerchief. If Ramirez was perspiring, I couldn't see it. I was ready to blame him for the heat.

"When did Lackland leave?" he asked.

"I don't know."

"Did you see which direction he went?"

I shrugged.

Ramirez stared at me again before closing his notebook with a quick flip of his wrist. "Thank you for your time, Mr. Carlson. If your memory improves, please give me a call." He handed me a business card, then nodded to Drainer.

I followed them to the door, determined to say something for Daniel.

"He didn't poison Washburn."

"Who didn't, Mr. Carlson?"

"Daniel Lackland."

"Why do you say that?"

"It's just not the sort of thing Daniel would do." The truth was, I identified with Daniel. Both our marriages tumbled after our wives started affairs with other men. Ever since Chris told me Daniel's story, I'd pictured Daniel as a brooder, like me, too repressed to consider revenge, too sensitive to get over the hurt. If I wouldn't do it, neither would Daniel. I thought about explaining this to Ramirez, a man who apparently read dogmatic theology in his spare time. I imagined him shaking his head and saying, "Only saints and fools argue from analogy. Which one are you, Mr. Carlson?"

What he actually said was, "I'll keep that in mind, Mr. Carlson."

I closed the door and faced an unpleasant memory of a hot day in mid-April, two years back. "What's up, Big Guy?" That's what C.J. had said as he climbed out from under my wife, Jocelyn. He picked up his clothes and added, "I guess you and your old lady have some talking to do." Then he walked out of the room, giving me a wink as he squeezed past me in the doorway. Jocelyn started to empathize with how badly I must feel. I stood on the threshold, listening to the slap, slap of the ceiling fan, afraid to move lest I fly into a thousand pieces.

CHAPTER★FIVE

Two hours later I sat at my small kitchen table, picking through the Sunday paper and the remains of a fried egg supper. The events at the reception played in my head like a continuous loop of film, narrated by Lieutenant Ramirez's questions. Was Daniel Lackland near the bar? Could he have heard who ordered the drink? When did he leave? Where did he go? I imagined Daniel, frozen like a deer in headlights, being interrogated by the detectives. He needed moral support more than I needed to finish the sports section.

Daniel and Chris' studio was in a district of factories and warehouses east of downtown. I took Santa Clara Street until it dead-ended at a barrier of battered concrete and a ten-foot drop-off into the river. I parked by a chain link fence surrounding an acre of blacktop where a couple of dozen school buses were rusting, the old kind with a hood stuck out in front of the windshield like a snout. Across the street and along the river stood a four-story building. In the blue glow from a streetlight I could make out a sliced orange in fading and chipped paint on the dark brown bricks. "Texas Sun" the letters read. The left side of the building dropped straight down to the tepid, silt-heavy water of the West Branch. I climbed the steps to the front door.

The short hallway inside ended at a padlocked metal door. To the right, a staircase rose into the building. To the left, a rendering of Michelangelo's David covered a second door. A bare light bulb illuminated a painted parchment over David's genitals. "If we're not here," said the message on the parchment, "hang around." I knocked on David's chest. When I didn't get an answer, I pushed on the door. The steel panel moved without making a sound. I let myself in.

The studio was a long room with a high ceiling, bare brick walls and an overhead bank of florescent lamps that lit the space like a convenience store. Opposite the door, a band of large windows faced the river. Two of the window panels were tipped open in a futile attempt to capture a breeze.

A worktable by the door held racks of paint tubes, each tube neatly capped, as well as several coffee cans full of clean brushes. Three nearby easels each cradled a small canvas not much bigger than a postcard. This had to be Daniel's work area.

I examined the first painting. It was a landscape, a broad West Texas vista of nearly flat land, broken only by a few mesquite trees. The ground was a subtle mix of gray, pink, yellow, and blue, giving the impression of brown or tan but without a speck of either. The picture drew me in toward a collection of tiny, red and black brush strokes that suggested a collapsed derrick or the empty frame of an abandoned building. As I turned away from the painting I felt a sad longing, as if I'd been looking at family pictures and recognized my own face in the features of some long dead relative. And I'm not even a native Texan.

At the other end of the studio, a square canvas, at least eight feet on a side, sat upright on a frame of two-by-fours. Three large patches of color, bright blue, red, and black, were painted one above the other like a stack of giant pillows. The size and color fit my image of Chris, but the composition and execution showed more planning and thought than I had expected.

I returned to Daniel's end of the room, looking for a pen and some paper to leave a message. I pulled a large notebook from behind a rack of paints and leafed through it. Each page had two three-by-five drawings, some in pencil, some in ink. The sketches at the beginning seemed to be studies for the sort of landscapes on the easels, along with still lifes of simple objects: bowls, cups and towels. Toward the end of the notebook the drawings changed character. The representational elements dropped away, leaving compositions of line, shade, and form that retained the sense of enormous space and aching emotion I found in Daniel's paintings.

I heard the outside door of the building slam shut. I stuffed the notebook back in its place.

"Howdy," I called out as the studio door opened.

"Shit," Chris exclaimed as he stepped into the room. "You scared the Jesus out of me. What are you doing here?"

"Sorry about that. I found the door open and I took the sign to mean wait inside."

"Yeah, no prob. I'm just thumbed on the edges."

"I came to see if I could give Daniel some support. The police talked to me a second time this afternoon. They think Daniel poisoned Washburn."

"More than think. Fucking arrested him. About an hour ago. I was just down at the jail. Won't let me see him till tomorrow." Chris kicked the metal door, slamming it shut. "Goddamn it. I can't believe they arrested Daniel."

He pulled two cans of supermarket beer from a small refrigerator and tossed one to me, then flung himself on a ragged coach. The beer smelled metallic, but at least it was cold. I poured some to the back of my throat as my mind flipped through a mental card file of people to call, actions to take. It was an old habit of ministry in response to emergencies like deaths, accidents, even arrests. Without asking myself if I should do anything at all for Daniel, I was already gathering information, making plans; as if there were something I could or should do.

"Where did it happen?"

"Right here," replied Chris. He held up a Tabasco bottle and shook some into the little opening in the top of his can; I declined. "I come back from the reception. Daniel's working, like nothing happened. Then the cops show up, about seven, flashing a fucking warrant. A whole hour, dumping shit out, pawing around. Ramirez and the fat guy. Make us stand off to the side. Real creep show, somebody plowing your stuff."

"What were they looking for?"

"Wouldn't tell me. I overheard a guy in blue overalls say

something about cyanide. They sealed some shit in plastic bags. I couldn't see what." Even sitting down Chris gave the impression of pacing the room, his knees pumping as if he could scuff away the intrusive memory of the detectives. "After they leave, Daniel starts lining up his paints. I tell him about the cops frying me at the reception. They wanted to know where he was every minute, like I'm his fucking babysitter. Daniel keeps sorting brushes like nothing happened.

"Then, boom, boom, boom, they come back with a couple of uniformed cops. Just like TV. 'Daniel Lackland, you're under arrest for the murder of Andrew Washburn. You have the right to remain silent.' The whole fucking thing. I ask Daniel if there's anything I can do. The young one, Ramirez, cuts me off, tells me to call Daniel's family. Then they put on the frigging cuffs, march him out. Two minutes. Finito."

Chris drained his beer and smashed the can between his hands. "Goddamn it!" He threw the empty against the bricks of the far wall. We listened to it ricochet and clatter to the floor.

"When did they question you?" he asked.

"About six thirty. They didn't ask much. Mostly wanted to know what happened at the reception. And at the bar the other night."

I tried to picture Daniel, quiet and careful Daniel, being led away in handcuffs. Being fingerprinted. Sitting in a jail cell. Chris must have read my mind.

"You ever been locked up?" he asked.

"Once, in Dallas. For blocking the steps of the Federal Building. We spent eighteen hours in jail."

"What was it like?"

"Nothing like real jail. There were twenty of us,

twelve women and eight men. They kept the eight of us together in a big holding cell. We prayed and sang hymns, shit like that. Some guy in the next cell tried to piss on us. That was the worst that happened. What about you?"

"Not even close. FBI grilled me once. I'd put a drawing of a dollar bill in a student art show."

"Was that you? I read about it."

"Yeah. They were afraid I'd buy a cup of coffee with it. Voted Best of Show."

We examined the wall again. I finally asked the question I'd been asking myself. "Do you think Daniel did it?"

"I hope not. You?"

"No." And it was true, I didn't think Daniel was capable of killing anyone. But much as I distrusted authority, I couldn't imagine Ramirez arresting Daniel without strong evidence. I kept that thought to myself.

"I think I'll try to visit him tomorrow," I said. "Did you get in touch with his family?"

"His mother'll be here tonight."

I nodded and stood up. "Did the police say anything about whether the poison was in the bottle or just the drink?"

"Nada. What's the difference?"

"I get my supplies from the bar at the Longhorn and I'm about the only person who drinks from the single malt scotches. If it was in the bottle, it might have been me convulsing on the floor."

"Shit."

I crushed my empty beer can and tossed it in the direction of the pile by the wall. The can was wide by three feet and flew out the open window. A few seconds later it plopped softly in river.

CHAPTER ★ SIX

I left the studio about ten o'clock. I knew the murder would be messing with my head the rest of the night, so I called Rusty Martin, who was on duty at the Longhorn. I asked him if Cheryl Lester, his girlfriend and a resident at St. Anselm's Hospital, would be stopping by later. Around eleven, he said.

I told him I needed a medical opinion.

Cheryl was sitting at the bar when I walked in. Underneath her white doctor's jacket she wore a Grateful Dead T-shirt. Her eyes appeared slightly larger than life through a pair of thick eyeglasses with clear plastic frames, and her brown hair was cut short enough to dry in five minutes; overall she has the air of someone who cares but has a long to-do list. Cheryl, Rusty, and I drive over to Arlington to see the Rangers play whenever we can. Every few months she interrogates me over lunch to make sure I'm taking my vitamins.

"I talked to the paramedics," she said as I sat down,

giving me a look of sisterly concern. "I hear you did a good job. When someone ingests a sizable dose of cyanide, there's not much hope."

"Thanks. That's what I wanted to ask you about. Cyanide, I mean. How it works, how much you need to kill somebody. I'm trying to get a handle on how this guy died."

"It's been a while since I worked in poison control." She traced her finger on the bar as if consulting an entry in a medical handbook. "Hydrocyanic acid is found in certain seeds and pits—peaches, apricots. But to poison someone you'd probably use potassium or sodium cyanide. They're white salts. You don't need much. I can look it up and let you know the lethal dose. It can poison you when you breathe in the gas, hydrogen cyanide, or when you ingest the salt or some other compound that produces the acid when it hits the stomach. It can also enter through the skin, but that's slower and less likely to be fatal."

"You'd drop the salt into somebody's drink?"

"You'd have to stir the drink. It would be easier to dissolve it in water and pour the solution into the drink. I don't think it has any color. It does have a characteristic bitter almond odor, although not everyone can smell it."

"So the almonds I smelled on Washburn's breath was really cyanide." A shiver rolled across my chest. The possibility that I had inhaled the poison drew me back to that afternoon: Washburn's arms flailing on the floor. A blue blush spreading on his cheeks. Spilled whiskey on his shirt, a stain as large as a plate. The smell of smoke and almonds filling the air. His empty breath scraping at his throat. My fingers filling his mouth and prying open his jaw.

At that moment, I felt Death standing behind me, there

in the bar, cold and unhurried, reaching slowly around me like a thief on the take or a lover about to catch me in her arms. A deep chill settled into my shoulders and the muscles along my spine. The skin on my arms tingled with the nearness. I thought of twirling on my stool and demanding an account for the lives of my mother and father. I imagined Death responding by enfolding me like coils of barbed wire that burned as dry ice. I wanted to look in the mirror across the bar to see Death's face, but didn't dare.

I stared down at the hump of a vein snaking over the ligaments on the back of my hand. "What if I breathed some in?" I said to Cheryl. "Should I get a test or something?"

"Don't worry. If you ingested enough cyanide to hurt you, you'd know it immediately. Have you had any nausea or dizziness?"

"No."

"Then you're fine." She squeezed my hand. At her touch, Death withdrew like a sudden, shrinking image on a switched-off TV, leaving only the cool air and muffled voices of a bar on a slow night. I looked in the mirror. Over the line of bottles I saw my own reflection, and behind that the glowing red letters of a Coors beer sign on the far wall. Something was there, I thought, and now it's gone. I knew I'd remember that silent presence for the rest of my life, like the face of a stranger glimpsed once and never forgotten.

"Your hands are freezing," she said, giving my fingers a brisk rub between her palms. "You sure you want to talk about this? Trying to resuscitate someone can be rough. The symptoms of shock can hang on for a few hours, even days."

"No, I'm okay. I deal with things better when I understand what's going on. Tell me what happens inside when
someone swallows cyanide."

"It prevents the blood from taking up oxygen. It's
called internal asphyxia. You keep breathing, but you
might as well be under water. The result is dizziness, rapid
breathing, headache, vomiting, fainting due to a drop in
blood pressure, convulsions. The effect is quick. If the
dosage is large enough, death can occur in a few minutes.
If the dose is small enough and you get to the patient soon
enough, you can usually treat the cyanosis successfully."

"If somebody swallows a really big dose, can you
pump their stomach?"

"Wouldn't make any difference. When it hits the stomach, the hydrogen cyanide is released and nothing can stop
it from getting into the blood." Cheryl looked at her watch.
Eleven thirty. She moved around behind the bar to help
Rusty clean up.

The Longhorn had emptied. I asked Rusty to pour me
a shot of Talisker, one of the single malts. A familiar, peaty
odor rose from the glass. Talisker is an odd scotch, with
more the oily feel of an Irish whiskey. But it still
reminded me of Glenfiddich. When Rusty and Cheryl
weren't looking, I leaned over the bar and poured the shot
down the drain.

"Thanks for letting me pick your brain," I said to
Cheryl.

"Anytime," she called. "Take two aspirin and I'll bill
you in the morning."

★

Back at my apartment, I propped open the door. Opened a beer, and examined the bookshelves. Now that I was reading sermons again, I had in mind something light. Maybe one of the Billies (Sunday or Graham), anything to shake the lingering hold of Death's visit. I chose Graham—not my politics, but an honest preacher with a straight-ahead, no doubts approach—and reclined in the chair with a sermon titled, "America's Immorality."

"You should no more allow sinful imaginations to accumulate in your mind and soul than you would let garbage accumulate in your living room."

My imagination wouldn't let me past the first page.

Internal asphyxia. One moment you're talking, breathing, standing on your feet. The next you're yanked down, a million miles from the people around you. You're a fish on a dock flapping your gills, but nothing happens. You try to breath and only gasp. You try to yell and you puke. If you're lucky, the cyanide pulls you down quickly. If you're not, you stare forever at the faces above you, your blood screaming for oxygen, your brain slamming against your skull. You know your thread's been cut and you are on your way out.

I pushed up from the chair like a kid leaping off the tracks seconds before an engine thunders by, and I crossed the short distance to the door in a bound. A breeze touched me and I discovered my shirt was soaked with sweat. An empty bottle dangled from my hand. I had drained the beer without knowing it. A few stars were visible through the haze of light tossed up by the city. The night air above the alley smelled of tar, dust, and hot oil from the chicken place. I could hear the hum and rumble of traffic out on

River Park Drive. My thoughts careened ahead. I remembered the policeman standing at the door of my childhood home, telling my mother that my father was killed instantly. Never knew what hit him. Crossing Mercer Street in downtown Milwaukee. Hit by a bus.

I had nightmares about my father, that he saw the bus coming. That he tried to get out of the way. In slow motion he felt the battering ram crush his body.

I longed to have someone there on the fire escape to hold me and tell me it was safe to go to sleep.

CHAPTER★Seven

I woke Monday morning determined to walk away from the visions and memories that had plagued me the day before. What's done is done, I told myself. You can't change it, so get on with life. Take a shower, visit a friend, go to work, serve a few beers, listen to some whooping and moaning, call it a day.

I also decided I was going to get my liquor and supplies back from the police so I could join the twentieth century and buy an air conditioner.

I phoned the county jail to find out about visiting. You have to make reservations. I signed up for eleven-thirty.

On the way downtown I bought a Clarion Arrow. A front-page story reported Andrew Washburn died under suspicious circumstances and Daniel Lackland, local artist, was being held; no news to me. There was a posed photo that made him look like a captain of the arts. The article sketched his professional life: author of a respected work on contemporary art; full professor for six years and dean of Fine Arts for four; avid collector of Western art; survived by his wife, Gwendolyn Shepherd Washburn. Gwen. I let myself recall sweat sliding over bare skin. Somewhere I read that sex is a small death; in the moment of crash and crescendo you cease to exist.

The Travis City business district consists of five or six blocks of tan brick buildings centered around Birdwell Park, where a tiny plot of weeds surrounds a battered, concrete replica of the cabin built by Joshua Birdwell (who came down with chicken pox on his way to the Alamo and arrived a week too late). He named the city for his fallen commander and the county for himself.

Two blocks north of the park is police headquarters. A young officer, a kid barely out of high school, asked me if I had an evidence receipt for the liquor and bar supplies. I told him no and he said there was nothing he could do. When I refused to leave, he went off somewhere and returned with a receipt. He promised to have the detectives working on the case get back to me about the supplies themselves.

In the one-block walk to the jail, a giant hatbox with slits in the side for windows, I sweated enough to stick my shirt to my skin. At the visitor processing window I was told I would have ten minutes. Only lawyers, clergy and immediate family get more time. I signed two forms, showed three pieces of identification, then followed an unsmiling sheriff's deputy—whose belt bristled with holstered gun, nightstick, and spray can of mace—down a pale green corridor. She unlocked a metal door that opened onto a pale green room divided by a floor to ceiling partition, glass on top, steel on the bottom. Three sets of

microphones were built into the partition. The deputy
motioned me to a folding chair in the middle. On my left,
a skinny woman—more of a girl, really—with yellow-
blond hair, black at the roots, argued with an older woman
behind the glass. The two were either sisters or
daughter/mother, sharing pockmarked skin, narrow green
eyes, and a pointed jaw. The older woman wore a blue
jumpsuit with COUNTY JAIL in yellow block letters on the
front and back. The younger one was dressed in cut-offs
and a Lynyrd Skynyrd T-shirt. Despite the heat
outside, I was wearing my work clothes: black slacks and
a white button-down shirt with the sleeves rolled up.

"How the hell am I s'posed to keep a baby?" the
younger woman whispered loudly into the microphone.
The room didn't exactly make for privacy. "I got me a job,
ya know. You 'spect Vernon to watch that baby, with his
leg 'n all?"

"Tammy, we're family," the older woman replied in a
tired voice. "If we don't got us, what else we got?
'Member that time you got pulled over . . ."

I looked straight ahead through the glass. Another
deputy, with the heavy jowled, disapproving face of a junior high principal, stared back at me from his position
behind the prisoners' chairs.

What am I doing here? I thought. I'm not Daniel's brother.
I'm hardly his friend. What moments before had seemed an
obvious act of kindness—visit Daniel, cheer him up—now
seemed incredibly presumptuous. I looked behind me to see
if the deputy who had brought me in was still there. No
luck. When I looked back at the glass, Daniel was entering
the room wearing his own COUNTY JAIL jumpsuit.

I jumped to my feet, and had to bend down to speak into the microphone.

"Daniel. Good to see you."

"Hello, Stu. Thanks. For coming." His voice sounded flatter and quieter than usual, though that was a fine distinction. His face was puffy, skin pale, and he had bags under his eyes. If he found it strange that his bartender was visiting him in jail, he didn't show it.

"No sweat," I said. "I just wanted to come by and see how you were doing. I figure this must be pretty rough."

"I'm okay."

"Chris told me your mother's in town. Did she get in to see you?"

Daniel nodded, staring down at his hands. For the first time, I noticed that he was wearing handcuffs.

"If there's anything I can do for her just let me know, okay?"

Another nod. I glanced at the two women. Tammy, the younger one, was crying now, while the older woman tried to calm her through the glass. I wondered how often the person in jail did the comforting.

"Everyone treating you okay?" I asked Daniel.

He leaned forward, his face almost on the glass. "What are they going to do to me? Am I going to die?"

"No. Absolutely not. I guarantee it." I responded out of instinct; solace first, reason later. "Do you have a lawyer?"

"I met him in court this morning. Stephen Fiorentino. A public defender."

"I'll go talk with him as soon as I leave here. Make sure everything's okay."

"Thanks, Stu. I appreciate it. Really." He settled back in his chair and began examining his hands again.

Something about Daniel—the way he exposed his feelings, the confusion and resignation that showed in his downcast eyes and sloped shoulders—made me want to protect him. I was beginning to understand why Chris provided chatty cover for Daniel in public, maybe even why Gwen married him. We sat awkwardly for a minute. I watched his hands. It dawned on me that he probably didn't know what to do with his fingers when they weren't holding a pencil or a paintbrush.

"Have you got anything to draw with? Will they let you have a pen and paper?"

Daniel straightened up a bit. "Crayons. They gave me crayons this morning. The guard said it was against the rules to leave me a pen or pencil. But that's okay. I haven't used crayons in years. You can get some really nice textures."

"I stopped by the studio last night. I saw the paintings you're working on. I think they're incredible."

"Really?"

"Definitely. The one with mesquite trees and that crumpled derrick in the distance was like to break my heart." Daniel was perking up, so I rambled on. "The colors are wonderful. I never realized how much pink and blue there is in dry land. And the feeling of space is amazing. I don't think the painting could have been stronger if it'd covered a whole wall."

"That's the one I picked. For the exhibition, I mean. Chris said he'd deliver it for me."

I thought about mentioning the more abstract drawings I had seen in the notebook, then decided against it. Daniel might not have wanted me looking through his notebook.

We sat quietly again for a minute, only this time more comfortably.

"I didn't do it," Daniel said, breaking the silence. "I hated Washburn. I'm even glad he's dead. But I didn't do it. I didn't put poison in his drink. I didn't keep a bottle of cyanide at the studio. I'd never do anything to hurt Gwen. We used to be married—she's his wife."

He stopped, having choked out the "W" word, and glanced at me much as he did when I examined one of his sketches in the Longhorn.

"I believe you."

Daniel's round face opened into a smile, as if convincing me were tantamount to an acquittal on all charges. It had been a long time since anyone put that much stock in what I thought, and I nervously examined my own hands, uncomfortable with the weight of Daniel's trust. I wanted to tell him that what I believed didn't make a damn bit of difference. But I kept my mouth shut.

I checked my watch. "I've only got a couple more minutes. Is there anything I can do for you?"

For the first time in our conversation, Daniel looked me square in the eye.

"Would you pray with me?" he asked.

Before I could reply, the older woman, the one on Daniel's side of the glass, leaned over and said something to him that I couldn't make out. He nodded. The woman looked at me, then bowed her head. The younger woman followed suit. So did Daniel.

I should have seen this coming. I don't advertise my former profession around the Longhorn, but I don't deny it either. If praying would lighten the load for Daniel and the two women, I was willing to pray. As I looked at the three bowed heads, I thought of a dozen old phrases—petition, confession, thanksgiving. But I had forgotten how to string them together; it was as if the words were in a language I had lost. In a flush of panic, I tried to remember a prayer I could repeat, any prayer.

"Our Father, who art in heaven . . ."

Chapter ★ Eight

The heat slapped me in the face as I stepped out of the jail. Even though I'd done my good deed for the day, I still felt uneasy. I'd spent a lot of time and effort the last two years pulling my life together, a life that didn't include asking God for anything. What grace we found at the Longhorn, we handed to each other.

It shouldn't make any difference, I told myself. Daniel asked me to pray. Big deal. I said the prayer and it's over. Oh, hell. Don't think about it.

I located the public defender's office on the third floor of the Wiley Building, a five-story brick, and stone office block across from Birdwell Park. The small waiting room had dingy white walls, worn gray carpet, ten chairs—and standing room only.

The receptionist sat behind a glass window. The rings on the pudgy fingers of her right hand each contained a word in raised gold letters, forming the phrase: "Jesus Christ Is Lord."

I announced myself. She spoke quietly into her handset, and told me to take a seat.

I pulled an old copy of *Field and Stream* off a coffee table and found an empty piece of wall to lean against. Several small children rooted through a cardboard box of toys in the corner. Most of the other people waiting were women, wives and girlfriends, I guessed. The public defender's clients were all in jail.

Half an hour later a man's head poked out from the doorway next to the receptionist window.

"Mr. Carlson?"

He held the door open for me.

"I'm Stephen Fiorentino." He was taller than me, the sort of person who probably grew up bending down to hear other people and keep from hitting his head. His brown suit was the same color as the armful of folders he was carrying. He freed a hand long enough to shake mine. I followed him down the hallway while we talked. "I can give you a couple of minutes. You wanted to talk about Daniel Lackland?"

"That's right. I'm a friend of Daniel's and I wanted to find out what's being done for him."

"What's being done, Mr. Carlson, is everything possible."

We moved into a small office. Stacks of paper covered every surface, including most of the floor. He added his folders to a pile on one of the two filing cabinets.

"I don't mean to be rude, but I have to be in court at two and I need to prepare. Is there anything specific you wanted to tell me?"

I hadn't thought of what to say. I'd simply wanted to impress him with the fact that someone cared what happened to Daniel. In the old days, whenever one of my parishioners was having trouble with the police or the power company or the IRS, I'd found that an expression of interest from a third party could make a difference. I decided to push him a little.

"I wanted to know if you or anyone else is trying to find out who really poisoned Andrew Washburn."

"I already told you," he said sharply. He stopped and rubbed his face. "It's Mr. Carlson, right?"

"That's right. Stu Carlson. Please, call me Stu."

"In the best of all possible worlds, Stu, I'd have a dozen investigators I could send out to find out what really happened. As it is, our office has only two. And right now they've got their hands full with the Delgado case.

"But let me assure you that Daniel Lackland is going to be well represented. We don't treat capital cases lightly. I can already see several possible defenses. In two or three weeks, I'll have one of our investigators start looking into the case. Nothing is going to change between now and then. The police have finished their investigation and we'll have access to all the evidence they collected."

He thought for a moment, then opened a folder and leafed through the sheets. "How do you know Daniel Lackland?"

"We met through my work. I tend bar at the Longhorn Lounge. Daniel's one of my regulars." That sounded thin, so I added, "I'm also a fan of his artwork. I visited him at the jail this morning."

"Are you the same Carlson who tried to resuscitate Washburn at the Artfest Reception?"

"That's me. I was running the bars."

"I'm sure I will want to talk with you before the trial. In the meantime, if you hear or see anything pertaining to

this case, please notify the police. It does Daniel no good
for you to keep information to yourself."

He glanced at his watch. I took the hint and stepped
out the door. But before I could leave, he spoke again.

"I know it's hard to have your friend sitting in jail. But
there's nothing we can do to get him out until the trial,
which won't be until mid-September, maybe October. See
those two stacks?" He nodded his head toward tall, twin
piles of brown folders. "Those are my cases. For each
case, there's someone locked up awaiting trial or on
appeal. I'm doing the best I can for all of them."

Across the street from the Wiley Building I found an
empty park bench in the shade of a rusting piece of steel
that was once modern art. A pigeon hopped in and out of
the harsh sunlight, pecking at the spilled contents of a
trash can. I remembered an article in yesterday's newspaper about a blackbird tumbling out of the sky, dead from
heat stroke.

I was trying to feel good about trying to help Daniel. I
found myself envying him a little for finding comfort in
prayer. That was me, once. I once knew in my bones that
God was at work in the world. That bedrock sense that
somebody's watching and caring proved to be a bridge of
sand. I went down hard. Even though I don't believe—
can't believe—I know believers are onto something.
Something that works for them.

I've known ministers who lost "it" and stayed in the
profession, figuring they could still do some good and

maybe bump into faith again. Not me, though. When something went missing inside, I could no more preach than a catfish can tap dance.

I threw a wad of newspaper at the pigeon, who flapped a few feet into the air and returned to her lunch. What's happening to me? I'm as introspective as the next failed cleric, but I don't usually sit on public benches in the scorching heat and catalog my shortcomings.

It was as if everywhere I turned, someone or something was trying to knock me off balance: The oppressive heat. News of Jocelyn's move. An invitation to preach. Sleeping with Gwen Washburn. Andrew Washburn's death. Memories of my parents. More heat. Daniel asking me to pray.

Maybe Bob the Prophet was right. Maybe the Hand Tools of God were coming to fix me. Wrench, hammer and drill.

I had to do something to get control of my life. But what? I had no power to end the heat wave and no intention of contacting Jocelyn. Seeing Gwen again was out of the question. There was no way I'd preach for John Hatcher.

That left Daniel.

CHAPTER ★ Nine

I delivered the police evidence receipt to the ArtFest office as an invoice. A guy with a purple mohawk cut me a check on the spot. It would cover paying Pauline and Steve, with enough left over for a cheap air conditioner.

I deposited the money on my way to Daniel and Chris' studio. When I knocked on the studio door, Chris shouted to come in. He was standing ten feet back from a big canvas, paintbrush in hand, inspecting his work.

"Ah, fuck it." He tossed the brush into a coffee can filled with paint thinner. "Wanna beer?"

"No thanks. I gotta work soon."

I sat on the old couch. He pulled a single can from the refrigerator and lowered himself to the floor.

"Hard to work without Daniel around." He took a long pull on the beer. "Saw him at the jail this afternoon. He told me you were there. Can you believe that talking-through-the-glass shit? Like he's carrying some kind of virus."

"It gets worse," I said. "I was just down at the public defender's office, talking to his lawyer. No one's going to be able to do a thing for two or three weeks. Even then I don't know how much they're going to do. So I might nose around some myself."

"You mean like investigate the murder?"

Investigate the murder—it had a forbidding, professional sound, like "irrigate the wound" or "probate the will."

"No. Just see what I can find out. Maybe get the police or his lawyer to pay more attention."

"Won't that piss them off?"

"It's not like I'm going to break any laws."

He took another drink and studied the can for a moment. "Makes sense, I guess. But what about the cyanide they found here?"

"The door's usually unlocked, isn't it? I could have hid an A-bomb in here the other day and you wouldn't know it."

"Shit. So if we'd had a lock, Daniel would be free? Fuck." He pounded his fist against the floor, and the dry pine boards rang. "A simple, fucking lock."

"It's not your fault."

"Yeah, I know." He swallowed some beer. "Can I do anything to help?"

"Tell me more about Daniel's marriage. I can't figure how someone who was married to him would end up with someone like Washburn."

"That's easy. Back in art school, Gwen was rebelling against her family. Wore beat-up painter's clothes and shit like that."

"She was in art school with you and Daniel?"

"Started the same year we did. Droped the MFA after a year and switched to Art History. That's how she met Washburn."

"Why didn't she go after a wild, artsy type? You know, somebody who dresses in black."

"Me? I'm too predictable. I figure she picked Daniel because a nerd bothers Mommy more than a hippie. Plus, our girl Gwen's ambitious as hell. She decided Daniel's on his way up, figured she can do a makeover on him, slick him up, buy him clothes, shit like that. Then Washburn came along." Chris slapped his hands. "She was outta there. He's got the kinda money she grew up with. He's moving up, hot-shit critic and collector, lots of connections. I guess she couldn't wait."

A knock sounded on the studio door. Before Chris could stand up, the door swung open and Gwen Washburn walked in. She was wearing khaki slacks and a dark, long sleeve blouse. She looked at me, then down at Chris, her eyes hidden behind black sunglasses. I think she blushed at seeing me, but it was hard to tell under her deep tan. I felt the blood rise in my cheeks.

"I'm sorry," she murmured, backing out of the room.

"Gwen," said Chris as he struggled to his feet. "Hello. Geez, I'm sorry about what happened. You know Stu? He's the one who . . ."

"Yes, I heard. Hello, Mr. Carlson. Thank you." Her hands made small patting motions for me to stay seated— or stay away. She looked at Chris and continued in a flustered, hurried tone. "I shouldn't be disturbing you. I came by to find out how Daniel was doing. I'll stop by another time." She closed the door on her last words.

I stared at the door, my guts tied in a knot of embarrassment, lust, and guilt. I had no right to expect her to acknowledge me or the night we spent together; those had been the ground rules when I invited her in. Still, I wanted at least a nod. Yet I was glad she hadn't, because another part of me wanted to pretend it hadn't happened.

Chris took a long drink of beer. "Fucking weird. Last place I expect her to show up."

"Are she and Daniel still in touch?"

"I think Daniel still talks to her. Far as I can tell, she never stopped liking him. Washburn was just a better deal. I haven't seen her here in the studio in a couple years, though. You don't think she and Daniel could have planned the murder together?"

"No," I said firmly, uncertain which one of them I wanted most to protect.

"Good," he said to himself. "That's good. Me neither. Just want to be sure."

I checked my watch and stood up. "I should get to work." Chris asked what I was going to do next. I mentioned talking to Pauline, and hurried out before I said something foolish about Gwen Washburn.

Chapter ★ Ten

I was trying hard not to think about women when I walked into the Longhorn and found a message from Jocelyn.

Stuart,

I understand John Springer told you I moved to Travis City. I hope we can be friends. I know you share my desire for healing and forgiveness. Yours in Christ,

Jocelyn

P.S. You work in an interesting place.

Goddamn John Springer! I crumbled the note and threw it in the trash on top of a pile of coffee grounds. Then I had a better idea. I retrieved the slip of paper, set it in an ashtray, and struck a match. In a few seconds only a curl of ash and the bite of fresh smoke remained.

Walter Jones, a retired Marine Corps sergeant and our daytime bartender, watched the display with his thick arms spread wide, palms down on the bar. A short, blue tie kept lonely vigil on his chest.

"Lady trouble?"

"My ex."

He nodded and gave me a rundown on the inventory in the bar, our usual routine for handing over the reins. He was a private man and treated others the same way.

I fought down the urge to ask Walter when she had left the message, how she had looked, whether she'd said anything. Harry arrived a few minutes later and took up his station at the end of the bar. I brought him the first of his usual four beers. He took one look at my face and decided not to greet me.

As the bar slowly filled up, I tried to keep myself occupied loading beer into the coolers and setting up. Unfortunately I had memorized Jocelyn's note.

"I know you share my desire for healing and forgiveness," I mumbled to myself as I chopped limes into halves, quarters, eighths. "I can bind my own wounds, thank you. Go heal yourself."

"Perhaps I came at a bad time."

I looked up from the cutting board. Gwen Washburn sat on a stool in front of me. She removed her sunglasses and set them on the bar. Her eyes were red; she'd been crying.

"Mrs. Washburn," I said, fumbling with a towel to wipe my hands. I didn't know if we were supposed to be acquaintances, strangers, or what, so I retreated to non-committal phrases of condolence. "I'm sorry about your husband. If there's anything I can do . . ." I extended my hand; she held it for a moment. She was wearing a wedding ring, now, and an engagement ring with the sort of diamond that people notice from across the room.

"Actually, I wanted to apologize. I stopped by the studio this afternoon on an impulse. You probably know Daniel Lackland and I used to be married. I left him, but I care about him. Even with what's happened. Do you think that's cruel?"

"Not necessarily."

She paused, then continued. "When I walked into the studio, I realized I'd made a mistake. It had nothing to do with you. I'm not sure why, but it's important to me that you understand."

"I do. There's no need to apologize. These can't be easy times for you."

"No, they're not."

She stared at me with the sort of direct attention you don't forget, both hard and open. She had looked at me that way the other night when we were finally naked, a searching, nothing-to-hide gaze that caught every scar and blemish. My impulse was to lead her to one of the booths and let her talk or cry or laugh or lean or whatever she needed to do. Only I didn't trust my instincts, not with Gwen.

"Can I get you something? A glass of wine? Some coffee?"

"Just ice water."

I filled a highball glass and handed it to her. A bead of sweat clung to the light fuzz on her upper lip.

"I also thought you would like to know about the funeral," she said. "Tomorrow morning. Eleven o'clock. St. George's Episcopal Church."

"Thanks. I'd like to be there."

She nodded and took a drink. The sweet tang of chopped limes hung in the air.

"I know this might sound strange, but which . . ." She waved her hand toward the rows of bottles behind the bar.

It took me a few seconds to realize she was asking about the bottle of scotch I used to pour her husband's final drink. I looked toward the end of the bar, where the back bar formed an "L" and attached to the front. The line of bottles continued around the corner, the last ones in easy reach of the person sitting on the end stool. That person was always Harry, so we didn't worry about anyone stealing the expensive booze.

"It's the green, triangular one," I said, pointing at the collection in front of Harry. "Glenfiddich. One of the single malts. Not many folks drink them besides me. Most people find the taste too strong. The police have the actual bottle, but that's what it looks like."

We regarded the bottles in silence. Gwen nodded and stood up. "I should go. Thank you again for what you did for Andrew." We shook hands; her fingers were chilled from the glass.

Through the set of longhorns painted on the front window, I could see Gwen climb into her car, a late-model, blue Mercedes. As it pulled away from the curb, I noticed Harry watching me watching her.

"Brown Eyed Girl?" he asked, tapping his left temple, the side of Gwen's good eye.

"I Can See For Miles and Miles," I replied.

I returned to the middle of the bar to blend a batch of margaritas for the happy-hour crowd. My feeling guilty about sleeping with Gwen didn't make her any less attractive. And having learned a little about her made me want to know more. Was she crying for herself or for her dead

husband? Did she forgive her mother after losing her eye?
Did she think Daniel was guilty? What did she love, hate,
eat for breakfast?

I told myself to leave her alone. Find someone safe.
Enjoy a little female attention. And don't sleep with anyone until she tells you her name.

Despite my own good advice, I couldn't stop thinking
about Gwen. It was more than her quirky beauty, the
sculpted cheekbones and empty eye. Her intensity—those
moments when she refused to hide—pulled on me like the
flame and crack of a bonfire. I rubbed my face with the
bar rag. Between unwanted anger at Jocelyn and misplaced desire for Gwen, part of me longed to recover my
old routine, my life.

I can still help Daniel, I assured myself. Focus on that
and the rest will sort itself out.

By seven o'clock, business had slowed enough for me to
pull Pauline aside.

"Can I talk to you about something?" I asked her.

"Anything you want, lamb chops."

I pulled some bills out of my wallet. "Here's what I
owe you for working the reception."

She took the money. She must have caught a serious
expression on my face. "Are you okay, Stu boy?"

"Yeah, I'm okay. I'm just trying to figure out what happened yesterday. I can't believe Daniel Lackland poisoned
Washburn. I thought you might have seen something."

Pauline described her movements, how her back was

to the bar while I was out getting more wine. Anyone—
including Daniel—could have put something in the drink
without her seeing it. She set the drinks on Washburn's
table before Gwen arrived; she remembered that because
she was returning to the bar when she noticed me watching Gwen walk in. She said Washburn's table had been
covered with empty glasses and plates; some of the people
standing nearby were using it to set down their drinks. At
least five minutes elapsed, long enough for her to pick up
and deliver two more orders before Washburn collapsed.

The rest of the evening was quiet. Eunice from KMart
complained about the heat and her stepson's pit bull. The
Rangers lost a slow game to Detroit. No reminders of murdered art professors or former spouses. I was beginning to
think the Holy Hand Tools had finished their repairs when
a short fellow—short as Andrew Washburn—took a stool
at the bar. I set a napkin on the bar in front of him.

"What can I get you?"

He squinted at the bottles at the end of the bar.

"Impressive collection. Highland Park, neat, water
back."

I was, of course, flattered that someone noticed my set
of single malts. On top of that he ordered my all-time
favorite, so I poured him a shot-and-a-half and set the
glass on the bar. As business wound down I was able to
look him over without being intrusive. I put him at forty-
five, maybe fifty; the only hair on his head was a gray
fringe above the ears, cut close to the scalp. He wore a

black shirt and slacks, well tailored to his pear-shaped body, and a single diamond stud in his left ear. He had sad eyes with heavy lids, like a cocker spaniel, and thick lips; a face that was more interesting than handsome.

I served him a second round at last call and began wiping off the bar. Pauline clocked out about eleven thirty. Harry left soon after to catch the eleven forty-five bus. The short man in black finally spoke.

"You're Stu Carlson?" he asked.

"Last time I checked my driver's license." I tried to place him. He was more stylish than most of our customers, so it wouldn't have been at the Longhorn.

"I'm Stephen Morris, a friend of Andrew Washburn." He extended his hand. "I wanted to meet the last man to kiss him."

It took me a moment to realize he wasn't hitting on me; he simply wanted to talk. I shook his hand quickly; he had a firm, dry grip.

"You knew him a long time?" I asked neutrally.

"Long, long, long. We were lovers, in the old days." He laughed, remembering something. "He was the love of my life and I hated his guts. Bartenders listen, don't they?" He held up his empty glass. "Do you mind?"

I shrugged, and served him another drink. I almost poured a Highland Park for myself, but I wasn't sure I could drink scotch and listen to stories about Andrew Washburn at the same time. I opened a beer instead.

"Did you know him?" he asked.

"I only saw him once, just before he died. Here in the bar, last Thursday."

"How was he dressed?"

"Suede jacket, string tie. He had a pin on his lapel, a silver lizard."

"That pin was his trademark. We found it in a village in the hills outside Mazatlan. Have you been to Mazatlan? You should go in March, when the forsythia are blooming. Andrew charmed the silversmith—he had quite good Spanish, better than mine. When the old man brought out the lizard, we both knew it was perfect.

"That was Andrew. A silver lizard. Smooth, polished, and poisonous. Gone before you could strike back. I remember one time in grad school, another grad student— a woman, Sarah something-or-other—beat him out for the job of cataloging the Orson Gallery's annual New Artist Show. Andrew didn't waste a moment. He started a rumor she was dealing cocaine. Gave an anonymous tip to the police. We sat in his car down the street and watched them raid her apartment. The gallery dropped her. The best part was a year later Andrew ended up hiring her to help him. She had no idea he'd cut her legs off. A shame, too; she probably had more talent than Andrew." He took a sip of scotch. "He scared the hell out of me. But I stayed with him. Laughed with him over his tricks. That's the way Andrew made you feel, that you were better than other people, deserved more. Until he stuck in the knife."

He studied the swirl of whiskey in the bottom of his glass.

"He was a chameleon. In California he was a Democrat. Here he's a Republican. I think in his heart he preferred men. Who knows? We were living in L.A. A lot of the dealers and collectors were gay. Andrew blended in. Maybe I was protective cover. We lasted less than a year after moving here. The art world in Texas is straight. And academics are positively puritan. Far better to sleep with a female student than touch another man."

"Why did you stay here after that?"

"I'm a big fish here. In L.A., I'd spend my life as an assistant gallery manager."

He handed me a business card from his breast pocket: Morris Gallery, Stephen Morris, Proprietor. In the old Gunworks building.

"Is that why Andrew came here, to be a big fish?" I asked.

"Mostly. He needed a place he could control."

I poured Stephen a fourth drink. He smiled his thanks.

"What was it like, trying to . . . trying to . . . save Andrew?" he asked.

I ran my finger across the edge of Stephen's business card as I described the convulsing body on the ballroom floor, the smell of whiskey and almonds, the scratch of his whiskers. "I'm a runner," I said, trying to find a way to explain what I'd felt. "When you're running, the world collapses down to the feeling of your body, the pumping of your legs, the air pouring in and out of your lungs. It was like that. I was aware of each breath I blew into his mouth, and each breath he didn't take."

"Did he say anything?"

"No. He was unconscious."

"Could you tell when he died?"

"No."

We were quiet for a while, thinking about death—or nothing at all.

"Do you believe in spirits?" he asked.

"I never gave it much thought." That was a lie. When Vern Walters, one of my parishioners, died, there were seven of us—his wife and sister, two sons, and their wives—squeezed into a tiny private room in Chesterfield County Hospital. Vern looked like a piece of driftwood against the starched pillowcase, gray and weathered and hollowed out. He had finished taking a sip from the straw Lois held to his mouth, when something happened. I've never tried to explain it to anyone, didn't talk about it afterwards with the family, though I could tell from their faces they saw it or felt it, too.

"I think Andrew's spirit is here, right now, with us," Stephen continued. "Or maybe it's his demon. Or his soul. For the first time, he doesn't know how to take advantage of the situation, the poor bastard." He held up his glass and saluted the air above my right shoulder. "Here's to you, lover boy." Stephen was crying, tears rolling freely from both eyes. He tossed back the scotch.

"Thanks for staying open." He dropped a fifty-dollar bill on the bar and walked out the door.

Chapter★Eleven

Over a breakfast of sour coffee and chocolate-glazed at Mister Donut, I tried to convince myself that attending the funeral would be no problem. I hadn't been in a church in two years. It's just a building, I told myself. You sit in the pew, you act respectful, you leave.

I paid my tab, pulled on my dark gray suit jacket and straightened my coal gray bow tie. Hazel Blaisdell, the oldest member of my congregation in Bloom, used to refer to this suit as my burying clothes. "You keep those burying clothes clean for me," she'd say. The shoulders and chest of the jacket felt tight. Maybe I'd put on a few pounds.

St. George's Episcopal Church sits on a leafy residential corner near the University. The well-watered lawn, perimeter of mature elm trees, and abundance of ivy reaching up to the dark wood cross at the peak of the roof gives the stone building an institutional air of old money. You feel that you should whisper even when you're outside, which is what the small clutch of dark-clad people on the sidewalk was doing.

I slipped into the back of the church. Midmorning light filtered through the deep reds and blues of the stained glass windows and speckled the unfinished granite of the nave. The heavy, rounded tones of Bach rolled through the sanctuary. Somewhere, an air conditioner pumped cool air.

I was gripped by an irrational fear that someone would demand to know why I was there. A few people turned to look as I accepted a bulletin from the usher. "He's the one, tried to save him," I heard someone whisper. When you're built like a human lighthouse, you get used to stares; but now I wished I were five-ten with a crew cut. From a pew in the middle of the church, Stephen Morris glanced back and acknowledged me with a tilt of the head.

I took a seat on the aisle near the back and calmed myself by inspecting the mourners. There were about a hundred people, evenly divided between art types, who had no trouble finding black to wear, and academics, in their darkest tweeds. Across the aisle from me, the young, blond woman who had stood beside Washburn at the reception sat alone and sobbed silently. The lover has no standing after death. Gwen Washburn sat in the front row, center aisle. I could see only the back of her black hat.

The closed coffin lay on a shrouded gurney in front of the altar. The coffin was dark reddish-brown, probably cherry wood, with an impossibly bright polish and tasteful brass fittings. I pictured Andrew Washburn's body inside, hair tucked in a neat ponytail surrounded by thick satin padding. I imagined the silver lizard pinned to his chest. The image closed around me; I had to stare at a stained glass window to fight off a wave of claustrophobia. It took me a few moments to work out the scene in the window — a pale blue Jesus holding out his open hands, a jumble of bright yellow fishes and loaves tumbling into the basket of a waiting disciple.

The priest, a scholarly looking man with sad eyes, opened the service solemnly, enunciating with exaggerated care in a way that was meant to assure, but which also seemed to distance him from any personal reaction. It occurred to me that the priest probably didn't know Washburn. Despite that, the priest was going to make sure we knew this was serious business. During seminary I developed categories of ideal religious experience: find Jesus in the sweaty embrace of Pentecostals; discover reason in the dry handshake of Unitarians; get organized with Methodists; get serious with Lutherans; make noise with National Baptists; be quiet with Friends; sip sherry and be civilized with Episcopalians; and drink whiskey and get real with Jesuits. I never figured out who I wanted to bury me. Of course, by then it wouldn't matter.

I went through the motions of standing, kneeling and praying, while my mind wandered off. I thought of funerals I had performed: Molly Hitchcock, aged one hundred and four. Walter Prescott Winslow, two days old. The Brooker twins, seventeen and a half. All held in the plain, white room that served as the sanctuary of the Bloom Christian Church. Folks seemed to appreciate the way I handled funerals, though I never knew if I was saying the right thing.

During a final piece of music — a young man and woman appeared in the choir loft to play Mozart on a violin and cello—Gwen turned and looked back along the aisle. A black veil hung from her hat and covered her face. I couldn't tell what she was looking at, maybe over my head at the musicians. As soon as she turned away, I slid out of the pew and pushed through the heavy oak doors at the back of the church.

The hot air outside gave me goose bumps. I stumbled on the top step, blinded by the glare, and then retreated to the shade of a large elm. I wanted to avoid Gwen. She scared me; I scared me.

I watched the church doors open with a soft suck and swish. The pallbearers trolleyed the casket down the handicapped-access ramp and over to the open hatch of the hearse. Gwen crossed from the church to a black limousine. She looked elegant and widow-like in her close fitting, short sleeve, black dress with a hemline below the knees.

Stephen Morris emerged from the church and joined me under the tree, wearing the same black shirt and slacks as last night. Maybe he had a closet full of identical clothes. We watched the line of cars follow the hearse around the corner. After the last car passed out of sight, I pulled the knot out of my bow tie and stripped off my suit coat. Stephen took a box of cigarettes out of his pocket and offered me one. I shook my head.

"You're right," he said. "Nasty habit."

We stared at the empty street. The sweet bite of tobacco drifted in the motionless air.

"Did she love him?" I asked.

"Interesting question. I didn't have much contact with Andrew after . . . well, for the last few years. I ran into them at an opening shortly before the wedding. He made a big show of kissing me on both cheeks in front of Gwen. I had the disturbing feeling he wanted to let her know he had other options. I only saw them together once after that, at a party. He was carrying on about a new painter he'd discovered. She contradicted him about how he described one of the paintings. She was right, too; I happened to know the painter's work and her comment cut to the bone. Andrew was furious but she seemed to enjoy it."

The young, blond woman emerged from the church and shielded her eyes. She looked in our direction, began walking in the other, then changed her mind.

"Hello," I said as she entered the circle of shade. "I'm Stu Carlson."

"I know," she said as she shook my hand. She was taller than I remembered, almost as tall as Gwen. Her puffy, bloodshot eyes looked out of place against the perfect halo of her hair.

"I'm Wendy Green. I was Dean Washburn's teaching assistant."

"This is Stephen Morris," I said. Stephen bowed slightly.

"Oh, I've heard of you. Andrew . . . Dean Washburn . . . thought highly of you."

"That's nice. I admired him, too."

"I just wanted to thank you for trying to save Dean Washburn's life," she said to me.

"You're welcome. I wish it had done some good."

She looked down, fresh tears in her eyes.

"Did you know him well?" I asked, giving her an opening. She probably hadn't been able to talk with many people about his death.

"I guess I did. He was . . ."

"Tell me something about him. I only met him once."

"Dean Washburn was brilliant." As I nodded encour-
agement, Wendy described the class and seminar she took
with Dean Washburn. I pieced together a picture of an
entertaining teacher with a propensity for provocative
opinion—his own—over substance.

"He loved to collect art," she said. "That's why he
mentioned you, Mr. Morris. He said you had a nice little
gallery."

"How sweet of him to say so."

"What did he collect?" I asked, ignoring Stephen.

"Mostly Western art, and some contemporary. Did you
know he had a Bodmer watercolor? He loaned it to the
Amon Carter up in Fort Worth. I actually helped Dr.
Washburn with his collecting."

"Really," said Stephen. "I didn't have a chance to speak
much with Andrew the past few years. What was he up to?"

"He hunted for art in places other people wouldn't
think of looking. Small towns. Down to Mexico. He recognized what paintings and statues were really worth, so
he was able to sell them for a lot more than he paid for
them. He spent a week in Monterrey last spring and found
some old bronzes."

"You got to help him with all this?" Stephen asked.

"I delivered some paintings to Dallas for him once,
when he couldn't get away."

"To Wallerstein or Western Arts?"

"No. I took them to a gallery that specializes in nineteenth century American. Up in Northside. It's called M.
Gregory."

"Fascinating," said Stephen. He gave me a knowing look, then curled his hand and gazed at his fingernails a moment.

"It's a shame he died," I said. "Why would anyone want to kill a man like that?"

"Did you know that Daniel Lackland was married to Andrew's wife, before she married Andrew? I wouldn't be surprised if she had something to do with it. I know for a fact she didn't appreciate him." She wiped a tear from her cheek.

"I'm sorry," I said.

I decided to back off; Wendy Green wasn't going to tell me much I didn't already know about who might have hated Andrew. She finished drying her eyes and smoothed an invisible wrinkle in her navy jumper.

"It's nothing you said. It's just that Andrew and I had a special relationship."

I took her hand. She squeezed mine.

"Please don't mention it to anyone," she said. "It was sort of a secret."

Her grip made my knuckles ache. Watching her struggle with grief choked me up, too. She had been the only person at the funeral obviously distraught; Gwen's face was hidden behind the veil. Most of the crowd was there out of obligation. Andrew Washburn had been dean of Fine Arts and that meant a certain number of colleagues and professional acquaintances would show up. I didn't see any tears other than Wendy's. I didn't hear anyone whisper "I can't believe it" or "goddamn it." Even if Andrew Washburn was as cruel as Stephen Morris described, no one should die so thinly mourned.

The moment passed. Wendy released my hand and said thank you in a voice I could barely hear. She walked away with quick, proper steps.

When she was out of sight, Stephen shook his head and clicked his tongue.

"Andrew. Reduced to sleeping with schoolgirls with perfect teeth who would believe anything he said. How sad. My one consolation is that I was probably his last man.

"You were kind to poor Wendy," he continued. "I'm afraid I've lost the knack." He pulled out a pair of expensive sunglasses, tiny, black circles on a black, wire frame.

"What was all that about the gallery in Dallas?"

Stephen laughed. "It's perfect. Andrew dealing with Gregory."

"Who's Gregory?"

"Max Gregory—if that's even his name—is as close to the real thing as a caffeine-free Diet Coke. His hair's definitely a rug. And that awful British accent. I know for a fact he's from Florida, probably Orlando. The only genuine thing about him is his mustache. He runs a glorified antique shop, passing off mass-market fluff from a hundred years ago as great works of art. I've heard from a reliable source that he does a side business in objects of dubious origin."

"You mean stolen?"

"Fakes, counterfeits, old masters with the paint still wet. Remember when the Getty discovered their prize 3000-year-old Koros was only fifty years old? It's a multi-million dollar business. Paintings, bronzes, stone sculptures." Stephen took a long pull on his cigarette, and puffed out three perfect smoke rings. "So Andrew was dealing in either knick-knacks or flim-flams. He always had a knack for finding and losing money."

"Your money?"

Stephen dropped his cigarette and ground it out with his heel. "My money, my first gallery, you name it. I trusted the little bastard. He left me with nothing. Never apologized. Never came by. Never called.

"I apologize. Midlife regrets. I was saying, Andrew was adept at getting his hands on cash. And just as good at spending it. He was always creating his own PR, trying to look like a player. He so much wanted real money, real art. Too bad he wasn't born wealthy. He had wonderful taste."

"How much is real money?"

"When you can bid half a million without looking in your checkbook, you have real money. Remember the Bodmer our little friend mentioned? That's real money. As to Andrew owning one to loan to the Amon Carter, preposterous. A line of drivel used to pick up art students."

Stephen lit another cigarette.

"I don't think Daniel Lackland murdered Andrew," I said.

"That would be good news. Lackland's one of the finest artists to come out of this little Texas town in a long time. I'd love to represent him, even if he's in prison. Do you know if he's signed with anyone? No, of course not. Tacky of me to bring it up."

Chapter ★ Twelve

I'd left my pickup down the block in the shade of a cottonwood. I sat in the cool driver's seat and watched people walk by, my thoughts drifting . . . Washburn . . . Gwen . . . Daniel.

Maybe it was time to give the police a stronger showing of concern for Daniel. I threw the truck into gear and drove around the block to a Conoco station. There was a pay phone inside the air-conditioned office.

Ramirez picked up on the second ring. I told him I wanted to talk about Daniel. I'd expected to have to argue; I didn't. Instead, he suggested we meet at two o'clock at a coffeehouse near the university.

When I arrived at the narrow, heavily forested cafe, Ramirez was sitting at a table near the back. As a concession to the heat, he had taken off his suit coat but not his tie. He was drinking espresso.

"You said you wanted to talk about the Washburn murder," he said as I sat down. "Is there something you remembered that you can tell us?"

"In a way. Did you know that they never lock the door at Daniel's studio? Anyone could have gone in there and planted cyanide in Daniel's stuff."

"What makes you think there was cyanide in the studio?"

"Chris Stark overheard the police technicians mention cyanide."

"Anything else?"

"From what I've heard, Andrew Washburn rubbed a lot of people the wrong way. Washburn had some kind of business with an art dealer in Dallas named Max Gregory. Apparently Gregory has a reputation for dealing counterfeit art."

"More?"

"No, that's it."

Ramirez sipped the thick, black fluid from his short cup.

"I appreciate your expression of concern, Mr. Carlson. We investigate all leads." He leaned back in his chair. "You interest me. I understand you were ordained and that you left the ministry."

"That's right."

"When I was younger I considered becoming a priest. I even attended seminary. After a year I discovered I was neither brave enough nor strong enough to be a priest. So I became a police officer. If you don't mind my asking, why did you give up?"

"The short story is my wife left me. I lost my faith."

"I apologize. I had no idea. To lose one's faith . . ."

"I get by."

Ramirez stared at me for a moment then stood up, his face returning to the neutral, professional mask. "You've talked to a great number of people, Mr. Carlson. I must warn you not to interfere with a police investigation." He picked his way through the foliage to the door.

I got up and got a mug of drip coffee. Back at the table, an ant started across the broad leaf of a rubber plant behind where Ramirez had been sitting. I didn't mind that he'd warned me off—but how dare he pity me? Ramirez had implied that while lack of strength and courage were humbling human weaknesses, loss of faith was a deep and unimaginable wound. Unimaginable for him, maybe. A Catholic can stray, and he will always be welcomed back home as a prodigal son. For Protestants like me, belonging is choice that can come undone. Just like a marriage.

Just like my marriage. Jocelyn had been so serious about herself, her God, her causes. Serious about me, too. She thought I had "great depth of spirit," though I lacked the discipline to realize it. After we met I began to see myself through her eyes, flattered and seduced by the certainty of her judgment. Her estimate of me became my estimate of myself, even though it fit like someone else's coat. So when I found her in our bed with another man, her faithlessness to me broke what faith I had in myself. The foundation cracked. The house collapsed.

The ant reached the edge of the leaf, waved its antenna in the air, and then headed back. "To lose one's faith . . ." Ramirez's words led straight into a question I'd only touched on the edges for the last two years. When I decided to go to seminary, I was convinced I had a calling to be a minister. Meeting and marrying Jocelyn only strengthened that conviction. So what happened? Did God stop calling on the day I walked in on Jocelyn and C.J.? Did I stop listening? I used to find comfort in the father who said to

Jesus, "I believe, help my unbelief." I couldn't even get
that far, couldn't say what I believed, if anything. Maybe
I had been fooling myself all along.

Without knowing it I had jumped to my feet, drawing
curious glances from the other patrons. I walked out of the
coffee shop, putting religion out of my mind by thinking
of what I could do for Daniel. Ramirez could warn me, but
he couldn't stop me. Maybe I should drive to Dallas the
next day and stir things up with M. Gregory; I doubted the
police would.

A more immediate priority was picking up an air conditioner at Appliance World before I reported to work at five.
But first I drove over to campus. The Angel of Parking was
watching over me; I found one of the few shaded spots
behind the library, a three-story cube sheathed in tan brick.
A woman with white hair who might have been anywhere
between thirty and sixty was sitting at the information desk
in the main reference room. She looked up from the journal
she was reading and stared at me over half-frame glasses.

"May I help you?"

"Could you tell me how I can find out about faculty
salaries?"

"I believe that information is confidential."

"I don't mean for individual faculty members. It's for
a paper on the cost of education. I need some ballparkfig-
ures on administrators and faculty here and at other col-
leges in Texas."

"You might try Marquardt's Academic Yearbook." She
returned her gaze to the *Journal of Library Sciences*.
"Over there." She pointed a long finger at a wall of reference books across the room.

Under the entry for Travis University, I found a salary range for deans from $45,000 to $70,000, not including the law or medical schools. So Washburn was making, at most, $70,000 a year. A princely sum compared to my wages, but not enough by itself to buy Gwen a new Mercedes.

Chapter ★ Thirteen

I had my back to the bar, loading bottles of Lone Star into the cooler, when I heard the voice, quiet and resolute.

"Are you Stuart Carlson?"

I turned to find a small, middle-aged woman in a simple, blue dress with long sleeves and a lace collar. She was thin, but not frail, and had short, gray hair and a round face with a few deep lines around her eyes and mouth. It was the sort of face that would disappear on a crowded bus. She stood in front of an empty stool, clutching a black purse like a shield.

"Are you Stuart Carlson?" she asked again.

"In person. How can I help you?"

"I'm Emily Lackland, Daniel's mother." She had the same slightly-wide-open brown eyes as her son, except that where Daniel's gaze sought approval, hers remained firm and skeptical. She looked to each side, then forced a smile. "I'm afraid I'm not very comfortable in bars."

"No reason you should be. I'm sorry about what happened to your son. Is there anything I can I do for you while you're in town?"

"No, thank you. I'm fine. I'm staying with my sister-in-law. Daniel tells me that you're his minister."

"That's right," I said, without hesitation. If Daniel wanted to calm his mother's worries this way, I could play along.

"You'll excuse my being forward," she said, "but this seems an odd place for a minister."

"Jesus made a habit of meeting people where they are." I was surprised by the conviction in my voice. "He ate dinner with tax collectors and talked to prostitutes on the street."

She examined my face. It wasn't the judgmental stare I'd received from fundamentalists; more the knowing acceptance of a person whose faith has lifted her through some tough times.

"Daniel spent most of his time here drawing," I said.

She nodded. "Well, I just wanted to thank you for helping my son. Please keep us in your prayers, Reverend Carlson."

"Thank you, Mrs. Lackland."

I extended my hand across the bar. She gave it a firm, quick shake, and walked quickly through the crowd gathering for happy hour and out the door.

"She raised him alone," Chris said. It was later that evening, the bar comfortably full of folks recovering from the day's heat. Bright splotches of orange paint on Chris' pale arms attested to a return to painting after Daniel's arrest. "His dad died when he was four or five. She took over the hardware store, raised her son, went to church."

He took a drink before continuing. "They're pretty tight. Daniel painted her portrait for her birthday. Whenever she visits, she's always picking at him like he was a little kid. But she's proud of him. Back in art school, she showed up for every exhibition. I'll be lucky if my fucking parents show up at my funeral."

"I went to Andrew Washburn's funeral this morning," I said.

"Big crowd?"

"Mostly colleagues. No one seemed too upset."

Pauline called for a pitcher of Lone Star. I filled the order, and brought Chris another beer.

"I talked to the blond student who was on Washburn's arm at the reception," I said, "—the one who went crazy when he collapsed. She was his graduate assistant and lover. She might have been the only person broken up over his death."

"You live by the sword, you fucking die by it."

I was reminded of Stephen Morris' description of Washburn as a silver lizard. It sounded as if Chris had some history with Washburn outside of Daniel. "He wasn't any Boy Scout," was all I said. "I thought I'd check into his art dealing tomorrow. Apparently he had some connection to a shady gallery in Dallas."

Chris shrugged as if that wouldn't surprise him.

"Do you know if Gwen has a job?" I asked.

"Not that I heard."

"Family money?"

"Shitload. Father's some famous surgeon in Houston.

But she doesn't have any of it. At least not when she was married to Daniel. Father's a millionaire and they're living on cans of fucking Chef Boy-R-Dee."

I could imagine Gwen turning down support from her parents. I decided not to mention her visit to the bar; even my public contacts with Gwen felt intimate and illicit.

"You think Gwen killed him?" asked Chris.

I had been avoiding the idea. But if Daniel didn't murder Washburn, someone else did. And she had ample reason to hate him. She had been near him at the reception before he took the drink.

"I don't know what to think," I said, refusing to go down that road. "Who knows that you keep your studio unlocked?"

"Gwen, of course. Friends. People stop by all the time. Shit, you found the fucking door open yesterday. Not anymore. Put a mother padlock on last night."

It was a little after midnight when I locked the back door of the Longhorn and stepped out into the alley. I was hoping to see Bob the Prophet; I wanted to ask him a question.

"Bob?" I said in a loud voice. "It's Stu. From the Longhorn."

I heard a noise from the dumpster down the alley. A head popped up, two large eyes under a red knit cap.

"Bob," I said, not sure if he even saw me. "I wanted to ask you about the hand tools."

"Nails! Have you seen the nails? The boards are cut, the hammers are hot. I must find the nails." He disappeared back into the dumpster.

Chapter★Fourteen

After leaving Bob in the alley, I pulled an oil-spotted city phone book from the glove compartment of my pickup and flipped through it by the light of a streetlamp. Andrew and Gwen Washburn were listed in Pecan Creek, an upscale neighborhood a couple of miles west of the university. You couldn't touch a piece of real estate in Pecan Creek for under $250,000.

I turned right on University Drive and headed west. The Washburn residence was in a row of Southwestern-style townhouses: stucco, with the second story set back in a fair imitation of an Indian Pueblo. The yard of number 215 was landscaped with river stones and exotic desert plants. Gwen's blue Mercedes sat in the driveway. A pair of white garbage sacks rested on the curb. The two upper windows were dark.

I scanned the street. No movement of curtains, no open doors, only a couple of upstairs lights on. What the hell. I stepped out of the truck and tossed both garbage sacks in the back. I drove home at twenty miles per hour, convinced a squad car would pull me over at any moment for theft of city property and invasion of privacy.

I sat under the bare lightbulb outside my apartment with a cold bottle of beer and untied one of the sacks. An odor of sour milk and overripe oranges rose from the opening. I took out a one-quart skim milk container, ten or fifteen empty cans of Diet Pepsi, coffee grounds, an empty vodka bottle, half a dozen empty yogurt cups, and the wrappers from at least as many Lean Cuisines. Gwen spent as much time cooking as I did. I imagined her in a kitchen with white counters and cabinets out of *Architectural Digest*, wearing a white robe, eating yogurt and smiling at her good life. Or sitting at a dark table with a tumbler of orange juice and vodka, mostly vodka, tears dropping onto the table. Does a glass eye cry?

I opened the second sack. Wadded tissue, tampon tubes, and dental floss. Plastic dry-cleaning bags, clothes labels, and a pair of nylons. A pile of old magazines— *Esquire* and *Vanity Fair*—and on the bottom, junk mail, catalogs, and two airplane tickets torn in half. Andrew Washburn and Wendy Green were to have flown to San Francisco in two weeks, returning four days later.

I leaned back against the wooden railing and listened to the muffled crashes of freight cars bumping and coupling in a distant railyard. Why was I pawing through the garbage of a woman whose husband was murdered two days earlier, who'd shared my bed three days before? Was I going to free Daniel by proving Gwen killed her husband? Or was it just that I couldn't leave her alone?

And why was I helping Daniel? It wasn't as if he were

my kid brother or childhood friend, someone I might launch a crusade for. He was a regular at the Longhorn, one of the crowd. I knew him better than some, not as well as others. I was his bartender, for Christ's sake.

The realization took a few minutes to settle in. When I left the ministry I thought I was leaving that entire life behind. But here I was, responding to Daniel the same way I had to members of my congregation back in Bloom. Whether it was a DUI, a miscarriage, or a lost job, I always jumped in, usually without looking. Like the night I tried to stop Hollis Conway from beating his wife, Priscilla, and walked away with forty stitches in my shoulder. Or the time I hocked my stereo to bail out Willy James. (I never saw Willy or the stereo again.) I never questioned whether I should do it, anymore than an out-fielder asks why he should catch a fly. You just field what comes your way.

Salvaging someone else's life can become addictive. It's one of the great temptations for a minister, the desire to play God. In seminary we practiced on each other, tinkering with our classmates' struggles over a broken relationship or a bad day in class. Ever on the lookout for someone we could shepherd back from the edge of the cliff. Ever eager to perform the unasked for good deed. Some people made sure everyone knew what sacrifices they were making for someone else, wanting to appear selfless and caring, no thought for themselves, stamped right from the mold of Jesus. Others did it for the power it gave them over the person they helped, a power all the greater for appearing humble and asking for no reward. Rarely was it ever about actually helping someone.

I caught my breath, surprised at the rush of feeling over those years in seminary. Those years with Jocelyn. That's when it hit me. Defending Daniel was a way to prove to Jocelyn that I could still be a pastor, that I could still care for my flock. And more than that, if I could show that Daniel had safely put his divorce in the past, then I could convince myself that I, too, didn't care anymore and that it didn't hurt, never had.

I wasn't doing it for Daniel at all.

Jocelyn didn't give up the ministry after our marriage fell apart. I don't know if she was a hypocrite or truly, deeply sorry for her sin. That was between her and God. The truth was, I resented that I had lost my vocation and she had kept hers. I wanted to blame her, but I knew I couldn't. It was between me and God.

Or me and me. I remembered something my Uncle Burky told me when he took me fishing the summer after my mother died. We were sitting in the boat, staring at our bobbers. He spoke without looking up: "The only person worth proving something to is yourself." It came out of the blue and went right back. It took me all these years to discover why he said it.

I buried the stolen sacks in the dumpster behind the hardware store and then climbed the stairs to install my new Polar Breeze.

CHAPTER★FIFTEEN

The air conditioner cooled my apartment but not my brain. That night I dreamed I was behind the bar, facing a hundred customers demanding Singapore Slings, Sidecars, Whiskey-a-Go-Go's, and more. I poured frantically—light rum, dark rum, sour mix, brandy. For each glass I filled, someone shouted for two more. The bar grew—a hundred yards, two hundred—and I was a dozen bartenders serving a thousand Andrew Washburns who barked and flapped dollar bills in my face. I didn't get a break until my alarm clock went off.

Over a bowl of corn flakes I decided to give myself one full day to help Daniel. If I got home from my nine a.m. visit to the jail by ten, I could make it to Dallas by noon, spend a couple of hours checking out M. Gregory, and be back in time for work.

I rehearsed a prayer on the way to the jail so I would-
n't be caught off guard. I was ushered into the pale green
visitor's room a little before ten. Except for the deputy
standing guard, Daniel and I were alone.

"Daniel. You look great."

The puffiness was gone from his face and his eyes
looked clear. He even had a slight tan, more than I had
ever seen on him. And he wasn't wearing handcuffs.

"You've been getting some exercise."

"Yes. They let me walk twice a day. On the roof. It's
sort of an outdoor gym."

"Your mother came to the bar yesterday."

"She told me. On the telephone last night." He looked
down at his hands. "I hope you don't mind my telling her
you're my minister. It's real important to her and you're
the only minister I know in Travis City. She said you had
a God-fearing face, even if you do work in a bar. That's
high praise from Mama."

"How is she holding up?" I asked to change the subject.
The phrase "God-fearing" conjured up biblical intimacy
with the Almighty Moses on the mountain, Job on the ash
heap, as well as the disturbing logic of snatching rat-
tlesnakes or proclaiming judgment on street corners.

"It's kind of hard for her. With the things people have
been saying about me. But she believes I didn't do it. And
she's been great, really, visiting every day. I know she
worries. Being away from the store."

"Have her give me a call if she needs anything."

"Thanks, Stu. That's nice of you."

Daniel studied his hands. I examined the outline of my
scalp reflected in the bulletproof glass that divided the room.

The deputy announced that we had one minute left. I thought Daniel would ask to pray. He didn't, and I wasn't about to bring it up.

"Been able to do any drawing?" I asked.

"All the time. They gave me some colored pencils. I've done portraits of the guards. One of them lent me a photograph of his kids to draw. I'll ask if I can show you. For the next time you visit."

"So you're doing okay?"

"You know, Stu, I sort of like being in jail. I get to draw. I don't have to worry about fixing meals or going to the store. If I could have my paints, it'd be perfect."

The deputy put his hand on Daniel's shoulder, and they left together.

As I waited for a sullen faced man in an armored booth to buzz the last door open so I could reenter the free world, I realized I resented Daniel coping, even thriving, in jail while I struggled with the odds and rare ends of life on the outside. And I was disappointed that he hadn't asked to pray. I'd rehearsed a nice little prayer, a bit for Daniel, a bit for me.

"Oh God, who brings down the prison walls, give us the strength to live our days and the peace to sleep our nights."

Chapter ★ Sixteen

Road trips across sweltering stretches of central Texas without air-conditioning are an acquired taste. With the windows rolled down, just enough air beat into my pickup to evaporate the sweat. A storm front was the only thing that would break the heat. I checked the rearview mirror for signs of thunderheads building in the west. Just thin, blue haze to the horizon. At times like this I imagine the sun-scoured hills and bluffs around Travis City as a setting for the Old Testament. The ground is baked to a blend of brown, tan, and gray green, and covered with a film of gray white dust. Briars cover the steeper slopes. Cottonwoods and elm cling to parched streams in the gullies and washes cut into the higher ground. An occasional farmhouse with stone walls and a tin roof sits in a field where someone still scrapes the dirt and tends a few head of cattle. It's the sort of place where bushes burn and folks wrestle angels.

The interstate hooks up with I-30 just west of Fort

Worth, a nice enough town—old neighborhoods, a few family-owned Mexican restaurants that haven't been spoiled by success, a university whose mascot is the horned toad.

Dallas is another story. It's the middle rung of a thousand corporate ladders, with miles of condominiums and eating establishments with names like Rasta Pasta and Baja Billy's. The sort of city that wears its money on its sleeve. There are churches in Big D with sanctuaries large enough to park the Goodyear blimp.

I threaded the interchanges and headed up the north tollway for about five miles, exiting onto a quiet, tree-lined boulevard with a strip of manicured bushes and ornamental trees down the middle. The leaves glistened on the trees from a midafternoon watering. The Northside shopping district consisted of three discreet blocks of Bellwood Drive: dress shops, a French bakery with an outdoor cafe, a small bookstore, an immaculate butcher's shop. M. Gregory Fine Arts was in the middle of the second block, across from the cafe. I parked the pickup in a two-story parking garage behind the block of stores containing the gallery.

I had no idea who bought "dubious" art. For the role, I had transformed myself into an extra-large version of Stephen Morris: black shoes and slacks topped with a black polo shirt, buttoned at the neck. Gay, vaguely artsy, wealthy, and not too bright. I checked the batteries on the small digital camera that I got free with a new checking account, then slipped it back into my pocket.

I ordered an iced cappuccino at the cafe across from M. Gregory and sat at a table where the lunch crowd gave me cover. During the next half hour no one entered or left the gallery. An old woman, bent and draped in an ancient, silver fur, stopped to examine something in the window. I had just decided to storm the beach when a man who resembled Stephen's description of Max Gregory walked out the front door: short, round, and a mustache like a blond whisk broom. He climbed into a white BMW with a vanity license plate that read "GRGORY" and drove off. So much the better. I left a hefty tip for the khaki-clad waitress and sauntered across the street.

M. Gregory's had a navy blue awning over the display window. A Mexican saddle, tanned to a deep mahogany and decked with silver, glittered under a spotlight. The gold leaf inscription on the tinted glass doors read, "M. Gregory, By Appointment." I checked my image in the glass; I looked like a parking valet.

The lobby was cool and dark, with a thick burgundy carpet. A young woman with too heavy glasses sat behind a low desk.

"May I help you?"

"Yes, I certainly hope so." I parked my sunglasses on top of my head and approached the desk. "Have I come to the right place? Is this Max Gregory's gallery? I'm told he's *the* person in Texas to buy art from."

"Mr. Gregory isn't here right now. I can make you an appointment for tomorrow."

"Tomorrow? No, no, that won't do. I have to have fly to Mazatlan at five. It's lovely this time of year—you should see it, wild with azaleas and no tourists. Anyway, I was hoping to find something nice for our place on Padre Island. A friend of mine . . . his name was Andrew

Washburn . . . may he rest in peace . . . perhaps you heard? Terrible tragedy. I was just at the funeral."

"A terrible tragedy. Professor Washburn was a great friend of the gallery."

"That's just what Andy was telling me, only last week, before that awful thing happened. Andy said go visit Max Gregory. He said Max Gregory has some very special works of art that I wouldn't find anywhere else. He promised to call ahead for me, but then, of course, you know what happened. So I thought I'd just drop in myself, on my way to the airport. Wolfy's waiting down in Mazatlan, so I don't dare miss the plane. Wolfy can get so mad. I don't know a thing about art, but I do love beautiful things. I especially love old American things, could die for Whistler's Mother, and I just adore Western art, Remington and that other fellow."

"Charles Russell?"

"That's the one. All those cowboys sitting around the campfire or rushing off on their horses and those Indians standing up on a cliff. I was telling Andy I wanted something like that over the fireplace at the new beach house. He said Max Gregory is the man to see. And now that Andy's gone I feel like his advice was a sort of last wish."

I busied myself inserting three sticks of gum, one at a time, into my mouth. "I just quit smoking. I have to do something with my mouth."

The woman stood up and held out her hand.

"Excuse me, I should have introduced myself. My name is Cynthia Taylor, Mr. Gregory's assistant. And you are?"

"Blaine Waters. But you can call me Blinky."

"Okay. Blinky. Professor Washburn was right. We have one of the finest collections of Western art available anywhere in the country. I would love to show you around."

She gestured toward a set of double oak doors that opened onto a large room furnished like an impossible den in a Ralph Lauren ad: maroon velvet wallpaper and bronze cowboys on dark oak tables. Individually lit paintings spotted the walls. On the far side of the room, a man sat in an armchair, leafing through a magazine. Light glinted off his scalp through a buzz haircut. He stood up when he saw us. His blue blazer was large enough to cover a table for eight. I put him at about thirty years and two hundred and eighty pounds, an alumnus of the University of Texas front line.

"That's Warren," she said. "Unfortunately even art galleries need security these days."

"I understand. We had to put a ten thousand dollar alarm system in the beach house. Something with little laser beams. Wolfy says it's state of the art."

"Is this where the special things are?" I asked, sweeping my hand around the room. "The ones Andy told me about?"

"Actually, we have another room with a few very unique pieces. I can't show them to you, but I can make an appointment for Mr. Gregory to show you, next time you're in Dallas."

"Why would you hide your best things?"

"These pieces are being sold by a Houston family who was forced to liquidate assets because of a downturn in the oil business. For reasons of family honor, they wish the sales to be handled discreetly, so we have avoided any public display."

"Oh, I understand. Maybe you could just give me a tiny peek."

"I'm afraid you would have to talk with Mr. Gregory. He's handling the works personally."

I looked at my watch. "I really need to be getting to the airport. But I wish I could get a sense of whether it's worth bringing Wolfy up."

She hesitated.

"Just a little one," I added. "Enough to get Wolfy interested."

She thought for moment and said, "I'll be right back." She went to the reception area and returned with a key.

"This way, Mr. Waters." She led me down a short hallway. She drew back a floor-to-ceiling curtain to reveal a door. As she unlocked it she looked over her shoulder and said, "It's okay, Warren, Mr. Gregory knows I'm doing this."

I turned to find Warren standing right behind me. I hadn't even heard him coming. I gave him my best more-rich-than-smart smile. I knew Cynthia was lying; I couldn't tell if Warren did.

Warren retreated to the entrance to the hallway. Cynthia opened the door while I fought down the feeling of being trapped.

The lights came on automatically as we stepped into the small room. There, on a pedestal in the middle of the room and under it's own spotlight, was a bronze figure of a Native American, a foot-and-a-half tall, his arms hanging at his side as if exhausted, his eyes looking into the distance. I pulled the camera out of my pocket, holding it in the palm of my left hand next to my leg to keep it out of sight. I hoped I had it pointing in the right direction as I took a couple of pictures.

"It's a Remington," said Cynthia in the hushed tone people use to make you know something is extra important. "It's called 'Far Vision.' It's one of a series he did of Indian scouts. Twenty of this particular sculpture were cast before the mold was broken. One is in the . . ."

A man's voice sounded from outside the room.

"I can't believe the gall of that woman," he twanged, "leaving me . . ." The voice stopped and M. Gregory appeared in the doorway.

"I told you never . . .," he started to say, then he noticed me.

"Pardon me," he said, holding out his hand. His accent shifted a thousand miles across the Atlantic. "Max Gregory."

He pumped my hand with his damp, fleshy fingers. His pinky bore a diamond that rivaled the stone on Gwen's engagement ring. He spotted the camera in my other hand and gave Cynthia a hard look.

"I was just going to ask your lovely assistant if I could take a picture to show Wolfy when I get back to Mazatlan," I said quickly, feeling my act wearing thin.

"Please, no photographs," said Gregory, moving between me and the sculpture.

"Sure, I understand," I said, as Gregory ushered me into the hallway. I slid the camera back into my pocket.

"Mr. Gregory, this is Blaine Waters," said Cynthia. "A friend of Andrew Washburn. Professor Washburn had recommended him to you—for the special works."

"Poor Andrew," he said, shaking his head. He kept looking at me, trying to place my face. For all I knew he might have been at the ArtFest reception and watched me thump on poor Andrew's chest.

"Perhaps we met before," he continued. "Do you by chance live in Dallas?"

"Los Angeles. Although as I was telling Cynthia, we're building a place down on Padre Island. I was at the funeral yesterday. Perhaps you saw me there."

"No, I couldn't make it to the funeral. Did you know Andrew well? I don't recall his ever mentioning you."

"I'm a friend from the Stephen Morris days."

"I see. Has Miss Taylor shown you the gallery?"

"Actually, she was just telling me about that lovely bronze in there."

"I'm afraid Miss Taylor was misinformed," he said, giving me an apologetic shrug. "Those works have already been sold."

Something had changed. Gregory either recognized me from Travis City or decided a real client wouldn't carry a cheap digital camera. His cold smile told that me he knew I was a fake

I looked at my watch. "I really need to get to the airport. Perhaps next time I'm in Dallas."

"Next time, then." He gave me another moist hand-shake. "And please call ahead."

He followed me to the door. Warren was right behind him.

I was halfway down the block when I looked back. Warren was standing outside the gallery. He was wearing wrap-around sunglasses that made him look like a Secret Service agent on steroids. He stared back at me.

I ducked into the bookstore and went to a rack of art books at the back, where I could see the door. A moment later, Warren walked in and occupied himself with some magazines at the front. I carried a large coffee table book of Cowboy Poet photographs to the counter.

"Will that be all?" asked the owner, a middle-aged woman who smelled of roses.

"Actually, do you have a restroom?" I asked.

She directed me to a door at the back. A short hallway led to the rear door. A sign in bright red letters warned, "Alarm will sound when opened." So much for that exit.

I peeked back into the store. Warren was saying something to the owner.

The hallway had two side doors. One was locked. The other opened into a combination restroom/utility closet. A small window above the toilet let in light from the alley. The window was wired for a burglar alarm. I had to hope the system was switched off.

By standing on the toilet I was able to open the latch and lift the window. No alarms, no shouting voices. I stuck out my head. The alley was empty and remarkably clean, each dumpster set in its own alcove. The pavement was six feet below. The parking garage was across the alley at the end of the block.

As I positioned a cleaning bucket upside down on the toilet seat, a knock sounded on the door.

"Is everything all right in there?" asked the owner.

"Fine, yes. I'll be right out." I didn't hear her walking away.

I climbed onto the bucket and managed to get one leg into the window, then the other. My hips squeezed through and I fell, bouncing like a load of groceries on the concrete. I ignored the pain in the leg where I landed and ran toward the parking garage.

I climbed into the pickup, tugged on an old Rangers cap, and threw the truck into gear. At the bottom of the ramp I saw Warren, half a block away, on the corner of Bellwood. He looked my direction. I turned the other way and headed south on back streets. I reached into my pocket; the camera was still there. After a couple of miles, when I was sure I wasn't being followed, I parked at a convenience store. My right pant leg was torn at the top of the thigh and the skin beneath was bright red. I could feel my knee begin to stiffen and swell.

I went into the store, filled up a tub labeled "Super Slurp" with iced tea, and picked out a bottle of iodine, a box of gauze bandages, a roll of medical tape, and a pack of Hostess Cupcakes. The clerk was too bored to notice my injuries.

Back in the truck I tore back the fabric of my pants and cleaned the wound.

As I started the two-hour drive back to Travis City, I wondered what, if anything, I had found out. The connection between Andrew Washburn and Gregory seemed too good not to mean something. And the way that Gregory reacted to my being in the room with the camera made me think he was hiding something. If anything came out on the two photos, I could show them to Stephen Morris, see if he could tell anything from them. But if Andrew was involved in a scam, what about Gwen? I told myself I needed to find out if she knew anything. Of course, that might have just been an excuse to see her again.

As the rush from escaping Warren wore off, I thought about Gregory's assistant and how she had probably already lost her job. Maybe I did her a favor getting her away from a fraud like Gregory. Or maybe not. Maybe Gregory was legitimate, maybe the bronze was real, maybe . . .

It was getting too hot to think. I opened the cupcakes.

Chapter ★ Seventeen

I arrived in Travis City at three thirty. I wasn't due at the Longhorn until six, so I stopped at my apartment to shower, change and redress my cuts. An hour later I parked in front of the Washburn townhouse. Gwen answered on the second ring.

"Yes?" She squinted to make me out in the late afternoon sun. She wore a large, man's white shirt, splattered with blue paint, and a ragged pair of painter's pants. Her hair was tied up under a red bandanna and some spots of blue speckled her cheeks and forehead. She was even more attractive dressed down than up.

"Oh, hello. I, ah . . ." She stepped back. "Please, come in."

"I hope it's okay that I came by."

"Of course. Excuse the mess." She led me across the entryway and into the living room. The furniture had been moved to the middle of the room and draped with canvas. Drop cloths covered the hardwood floor. Two walls were already coated in a deep, royal blue, the rest still a pale yellow. Gwen wouldn't be the first person to paint or wall-paper or move furniture after someone dies, although she got around to it a little sooner than most. Recast the room to ward off the ghosts.

She pulled the canvas off two straight back chairs; I accepted one, she sat in the other. She seemed at ease amid the rollers, brushes, and cans of paint. For the first time, I could picture her in an art studio.

"To what do I owe this visit?" she asked. At the door she had been bewildered at my unannounced arrival. And for a brief moment I sensed the tension I'd felt when she visited the bar two days earlier. But now her manner was distant and courteous, as if I was a neighbor stopping by with condolences and a casserole.

"I wanted to see how you were doing," I said.

"Fine, thank you. I'm keeping myself busy. Would you like something to drink?" It sounded like a rhetorical question.

"No, thank you. Is there anything I can do? Anything you need?"

"No, I'm fine. Thank you for offering."

She put her hands on the tops of her legs, signaling that my concern was noted and she was ready to stand up and show me out. I told myself to say goodbye, back off, let her be a widow. But I couldn't keep my distance.

"There was something I wanted to ask you," I said.

Her eyes widened in a moment of panic and she held up her hand as if trying to quiet me. "Listen, if it's about the other night . . ."

"No, nothing like. I was wondering about something your husband told me."

She paused and crossed her arms defensively. "I didn't realize you knew Andrew."

"People talk to bartenders." I was guessing that Washburn often went out without Gwen, so she'd have no way to disprove my story. "He came in to the Longhorn once and told me about how he'd go out to auctions and small towns to buy paintings and sculptures, then resell them."

Gwen stared at me, her good eye no more expressive than the glass one.

"I asked him how he sold the stuff, like auctions or ads in the papers. He told me that he sold them through a gallery in Dallas called M. Gregory."

Gwen's face and arms tensed at the mention of the gallery. Her voice stayed even and measured. "My husband had many dealings in the art world."

I nodded and continued, too far along to go back now. "Well, I was up in Dallas the other day and happened to drive past M. Gregory, so I stopped to see what sort of art they had. You won't believe this, but I think they sell fake art. You know, paintings and sculptures made to look like the real thing."

"Are you suggesting that Andrew . . ."

"Oh, no. I was afraid he might have bought some himself."

"My husband had better judgment than that." Her voice had an edge like an axe. I'd crossed a line and we both knew it. "And I don't appreciate you prying into his affairs."

"I'm sorry." I rose from my seat. "I didn't mean to be nosey. I just thought you'd want to know. I'll get out of your hair." I turned and walked quickly to the door, letting myself out before she had a chance to say anything else.

I drove the pickup around the corner, parked along the curb, and slapped my head a few times. You dumb shit. She sleeps with you three days before her husband's murdered. So how's she going to feel when you show up at her house? And what did you accomplish? She's heard of Gregory. Big deal. You've stolen her garbage and been thrown out of her house. She'll never want to see you again and Daniel's no closer to getting out of jail.

I was still kicking my own metaphorical butt when Gwen emerged from the townhouse, still in painting clothes, and backed the blue Mercedes out of the driveway. I quickly pulled an old newspaper in front of my face as she went past, going the opposite direction. I only hesitated a moment before doing a three-point turn and tagging along.

She was a block ahead when she stopped at the light on Pecan Creek Drive. I let a station wagon full of screaming kids get in front of me. She went through the intersection, then took the left fork where the road splits and becomes Tumble Lake Road. After two or three miles the residential streets gave way to a few old farmhouses and then to a strip of bait shops, liquor stores, and boat dealers. Signs along the road indicated turnoffs for boat launchings and picnic areas on Tumble Lake, a shallow, sprawling lake that's warm as a bath in summer, good for catfish, skinny dippers, and three or four drownings a season.

Gwen swung off the highway onto an unmarked black-top road. I pulled the pickup into a stall in a do-it-yourself car wash and watched the blue sedan glide across open fields the color of old bone and disappear over a rise. I bought a couple of cans of Dr. Pepper out of a soda machine that shuddered every few seconds as its compressor struggled to wring some cold from the tight fisted heat.

The road must run down to Tumble Lake, probably to some cottages. I could let her get wherever she was going, then drive down the road looking for her car. I finished the first Dr. Pepper, then set out.

The blacktop road crossed a small ridge, then dropped down toward a thin forest of cottonwood and elm. I followed the road along the edge of the woods, catching glimpses of the lake a quarter mile off to the right through breaks in the trees. Every hundred yards a collection of wooden nameplates nailed to a tree identified a dirt road leading down to summer cottages. Two names, Johnson and Washburn, marked the third road. I drove the truck another quarter mile along the blacktop road and parked behind a clump of bushes where someone had burned a pile of trash, then set out on foot through the trees. A couple of kids on jet skis were hotdogging somewhere nearby on the water, the incessant revving of the motors covering any noise I made in the dry leaves and underbrush.

I stopped on the crest of small hill overlooking a low building surrounded by a screened-in porch on three sides. Strips of dull, green moss etched the joints in the corrugated tin roof. A small plot of dead grass led to a dock that stretched twenty feet over dry, cracked lakebed; the water level had been lowered to provide drought relief for farmers downstream. On the other side of the house sat a garage or storage shed, covered with the same dark-stained wood shingles as the house but with a newer roof of light green fiberglass. The wooden doors of the shed were ajar. The blue Mercedes was parked on a nearby bed of gravel.

I settled in with my back against a tree, my body hidden by a rotting log. For the next five minutes the sound of intermittent pounding came from the shed, then Gwen emerged. She swung the doors shut, threaded a chain through the handles, and closed a padlock on the ends of the chain. She glanced around quickly, then climbed into the Mercedes and drove away.

Alone with the heat and my sore leg, I decided that I might as well finish what I'd started; it couldn't make things any worse. I didn't have any tools in my truck that could cut through a chain. But I did at my apartment. And I had plenty of time tomorrow for a return visit.

I limped back up the hill, my knee complaining with each step. I opened the second Dr. Pepper and headed the truck toward town. After cleaning up and changing clothes, I stopped at a drugstore to print out the photos I took at Gregory's. One of them was completely blurred, but the other showed the sculpture clearly, though from the odd angle of looking up. I put the prints in the glove compartment of my pickup and left the camera on the seat.

When I arrived at the Longhorn for work, the police were waiting.

Chapter ⋆ Eighteen

"These fellows want to talk with you," Rusty announced, flipping his chopped, blond hair toward Ramirez and Drainer. The bar was half-full, folks stopping off on the way home.

I motioned the detectives over to an empty booth. Ramirez chose a table instead. He sat with his back to the light from the door. I shifted my chair to sit in a patch of shadow.

"What can I do for you?" I asked, easing myself into the chair with my sore knee.

"Mr. Carlson, did you visit Gwen Washburn this afternoon?"

"Yes. I wanted to offer her my condolences."

"We received a call from her. She said you were questioning her about her husband's business." He stared at me for a moment, his eyes steel gray in the shadows of his face. I pictured Gwen sitting across from me at the townhouse and her sudden flight to the lake house. It had struck me as a challenge, part of a game that only I knew we were playing. Or so I thought.

"Why did you go to Mrs. Washburn's house, Mr. Carlson?" he asked.

"I told you, I went to offer my condolences. I mentioned meeting her husband here in the Longhorn. Something about it upset her, so I apologized and left."

Ramirez consulted his notebook before changing topics. I decided Gwen must not have seen me at the lake. Or at least she hadn't reported it to the police.

"We also know," he said, "that you spoke with Daniel Lackland's attorney and visited Lackland twice at the jail."

I shrugged. Stephen Fiorentino wouldn't have mentioned my visit; Daniel must have volunteered the information.

"Mr. Carlson, we have spoken about this before. It is a criminal offense to interfere with a police investigation."

I gave him a blank look. There was no way I could tell him about my visit to M. Gregory; that would only confirm his judgment of my actions, my calling, my life. I needed to prove him wrong. If not about me, then at least about Daniel's guilt.

"You are not to go near Mrs. Washburn again," he said. "And if I hear that you have been bothering witnesses or anyone else involved in this case, I will have you arrested. Do we understand each other?"

"Sure."

Ramirez waited a full minute, then got up from the table. "Take care of that leg," he said, and walked out. Drainer pushed up from the table and trudged after.

"Some kind of trouble?" Rusty asked.

"No. They're just doing their jobs." And I meant it. Ramirez had done me a favor. Any doubts I had about breaking into the shed were gone.

For a couple of hours I felt okay, even to the point of laughing at myself as I told Chris about my misadventures in Dallas. Then Rusty called me to the telephone.

"Somebody named Jocelyn," he said, cupping his hand over the mouthpiece. "I forgot to tell you she called earlier."

I backed away as if Rusty had produced a rattlesnake.

"I'm not here. I'm gone. Tell her I went to pick up some beer."

I tripped over a case of beer and landed bottom down in a puddle of beer. Louise and some of the other regulars applauded.

"I'm sorry," said Rusty into the telephone. "He left a few minutes ago. He had to pick up a beer shipment. We go through a lot of beer down here."

I mumbled something about the Ex-Wife from Hell, then retreated to the end of the bar, trying to dry the seat of my pants without attracting any more attention. Sooner or later I had to confront Jocelyn. I just wasn't ready.

Harry looked up.

"Raindrops keep falling on my head," he offered.

"Just like a guy whose feet are too big for his bed," I replied, reaching for another dry towel.

"Nothing seems to fit," he continued.

"So I'm never gonna stop the rain by complaining."

I laughed. Harry, as always, was right. Later, when business slowed, I had time to make my own phone call: Stephen Morris' business card listed a night number.

"What a pleasant surprise," he said when I introduced myself.

"I hope so." I described my visit to M. Gregory and told him I could bring the photo by his gallery.

"You have been a busy camper. I don't need to see the photo to tell you the bronze is a notorious fake. I should know; I bought one of them once. I managed to recover most of what I paid for it, but I was still out over five thousand dollars. There were twenty of the bronzes cast, but the other seventeen were melted down at the foundry in a dispute with Remington over payment. The only three known authentic castings are in museums. Copies of the bronze surface regularly, with the seller claiming them to be one of the 'lost scouts.'"

"How much do they go for?"

"It probably costs five hundred dollars to make, maybe a thousand, at a foundry down in Mexico. They sell up here for twenty to fifty thousand. I paid thirty myself.

I thought of one more question. "Was Gregory at the Artfest reception?"

"I believe he was. I wonder if he recognized you."

"So do I."

By midnight we were down to three booths and a few stools at the bar. I poured a cup of coffee and propped myself against the back bar. Someone had pumped quarters into the jukebox and pressed every Patsy Cline song on the list. "I fall to pieces. Each time I see you again." Good music for thinking about the wrong women.

There was Jocelyn. She had definite ideas on the way a caring, sensitive minister acts. Every week, when I returned from Bloom to the small house we kept in Chesterfield, she wanted to know how I'd performed. So I'd tell her about splitting a bottle of Seagram's with Hollis Conway and his brother, Earl, while not catching fish. Or watching soaps all morning in Francine Carter's trailer. I did those things because that's the way my congregation lived. I also took a secret, wicked joy in reporting to Jocelyn and catching her stern expression of disapproval. Maybe I was as wrong for Jocelyn as she was for me.

Then there was Gwen. When she looked at me with her one good eye that night in my apartment, she didn't see anyone else. Just me, a tall, bald bartender. I'd taken a wrong turn with her, although I'm not sure there was a right one. Maybe Patsy's right: "I'm crazy for trying. Crazy for crying."

An hour later I locked up the back door to the Longhorn and walked down the alley. I spotted the smashed windows on my truck from half a block away, the fractures in the glass glittering under the streetlamp. The windshield had been hit four times; somehow the smashed glass had remained intact. The driver's window had exploded inward, except for a few splinters poking up from the bottom of the frame. The camera I'd left on the seat was gone. I checked the glove compartment; the photos were still there. Maybe it was a simple robbery, hit and run. Though that didn't explain busting every window.

I used an old towel to knock the remaining glass out of the driver's window and sweep the shards off the seat. By bending down and leaning to the right I found enough clear windshield to drive home. Back at the apartment I fixed an ice pack for my knee, opened a beer, and sat on the top step, looking down at my wounded pickup. I was so tired and the day had been so full that I couldn't quite believe it had happened. I told myself it was a simple burglary, anonymous, random, a target of opportunity. Not someone who had come all the way from Dallas to make sure my camera didn't have any unwanted pictures.

Before going to bed I locked the door and set my three cacti, Shadrach, Meshach, and Abednego, in the middle of the floor.

CHAPTER★Nineteen

In the daylight the shattered glass seemed less threatening, more likely an act of thief and vandalism than a message from a vengeful gallery owner. I spent the morning at J&B Auto Glass on Old Fort Worth Highway. They replaced the two windows on my truck for $110 while I sat under a fan in their un-air-conditioned waiting room.

Back at my apartment I loaded my entire collection of tools—crowbar, hacksaw, hammer, bolt cutter, duct tape, flashlight, jar of nails, and three screwdrivers—into an old, canvas duffel bag. I stopped at Mister Donut for an early lunch of raspberry jelly bismarks and black coffee, then Wal-Mart for a cheap, disposable 35 mm camera.

Twenty minutes later I parked the truck behind the same stand of bushes along the Tumble Lake access road where I'd parked the day before. There were no speed-boats or jet skis on the lake; my steps through the dead leaves sounded like Godzilla stomping Tokyo. I stopped on the hill above the house. The gravel parking area was

vacant, the house appeared closed up. I waited a moment
to assure myself that no one was around. The heat hugged
me like a drunken uncle. A tangle of poison ivy at my feet
filled the air with a thick, stinging vegetable odor.

I picked my way down the short slope. The shed,
really more of a small garage, had windows on either side,
with an air conditioner humming in one. I peered in the
other window, but caught only my reflection; the glass had
been painted over on the inside.

The front of the shed had double wooden doors that
swung out. A length of one-inch link chain was wrapped
tightly around the U-shaped metal handles. A padlock, the
kind you see on television holding together as a bullet
slams through it in slow motion, secured the ends of the
chain. Fortunately the Washburns had hooked a premium
lock to a bargain chain with links welded from quarter-
inch rods.

I looked around one more time, checking for witnesses
and steeling myself for the deed. Don't worry, I told
myself. You've been arrested for a good cause before. Get
to work.

I snapped one side of a link on my second try and had
the chain off and the door open within a minute. Cool air,
scented with fresh sawdust, rolled out of the shadows. I
slipped inside and pulled on the string to the overhead
light. The room was eight feet on a side and partially finished: gray, all-weather carpet glued to the concrete floor,
bare Sheetrock on the walls, and the framework for a ceiling installed, with no tiles hung—although rolls of pink
insulation had been carefully wedged between the rafters
under the roof. Electric baseboard heating had been

installed along two walls. Someone had made sure this room stayed cozy, winter or summer. Another day or two of work and the shed would have been a nice study or small guestroom. But the Sheetrock wasn't new; it had been up for several years. A small workbench on the far wall contained a set of hand tools, a measuring tape, and a circular saw, but no spackling compound or plaster, no ceiling tiles. A sprinkling of yellow sawdust coated an older, graying pile on the carpet under the workbench.

The only other furnishings in the shed were two large, wooden boxes, three feet by four feet and a foot deep, set on end, and a supply of white pine one-by-twos and one-by-fours similar to those used for the boxes. One crate was newly built, the cut ends were still raw, while the other crate was a bit older, but not weathered. Neither possessed markings of any kind, no shipping labels or content lists. The newer crate had no cover and was empty, except for some sort of wooden frame or rack on the inside. The cover of the older crate was screwed down tight.

I removed one screw by hand and was straining on a second when I noticed the power screwdriver on the workbench. The screws backed out smoothly and the cover came off as neatly as the lid on a cookie jar. I lifted out an inch-thick piece of foam insulation that covered the contents.

The built-in rack held two unframed paintings. A third slot was empty. I pulled out one of the paintings. It was a vast panorama of the Rocky Mountains with an Indian encampment on a green meadow in the foreground. My foggy recollection of an American Art survey course in college told me it was by Bierstadt or Cole or some other

nineteenth century American landscape painter. I looked
back in the crate. The other painting was identical, down
to the web of fine cracks and lines spread across the surface of the paint.

I knelt to examine the back of the painting. It seemed
to have been painted on old canvas. I sniffed the surface;
a slight scent of dust and dry mold. I turned it over and
sniffed the front. If the painting weren't identical with the
one still in the crate and there hadn't been a faint smell of
linseed oil or varnish, I'd have sworn it was over a hundred years old.

I shifted the painting to pick up more light from the
weak, 40-watt bulb hanging from the ceiling. A golden
glow from an unseen sunrise or sunset etched the jagged
ridge of a line of mountains. At the base of the mountains,
still in deep shadows, a dark stream wandered across a
valley as green and smooth as a fairway. Three tiny figures, almost lost in the twilight and dwarfed by the peaks,
surrounded a teepee in the foreground, the only sign of
human life. I wondered if it was a copy of an actual painting, or just "in the style" of some famous artist.

How long would it take to paint one of these? I examined the tiny brush strokes that formed a tree. A week? A
month? Although the style was different, I knew only one
painter with such a fine, meticulous technique. Could
Daniel have been forging paintings for Washburn? Why
would he do that? Money? Daniel didn't care about
money, only art. Blackmail? I tried and failed to imagine
Daniel doing something shameful enough to blackmail.
For all I knew, Washburn picked up the forged paintings in
Mexico.

Here was some physical evidence that might link Andrew Washburn to Gregory's scam. I could photograph the paintings, put them back in the case, and screw down the top. If I took the circular saw, the break-in would look like a robbery. Then Stephen Morris could verify what I'd found and I could send the photos to the police. Anonymously.

I stepped outside and shielded my eyes. The direct sun was too bright for a decent picture. The thick foliage of a cottonwood tree near the house provided the only shelter from the overhead glare of the sun. I retrieved the painting from inside the shed and carried it across the yard. Fresh sweat dripped down my chest from the short walk. I leaned the painting against the tree and stepped back to find the best angle for the photo.

I almost didn't hear the crunch of tires on the dirt road.

Chapter ★ Twenty

Beyond the corner of the shed I glimpsed a white car moving through the trees. I ran in the direction of the lake house, keeping the shed between the approaching automobile and myself. The camera slipped from my hand, bounced, and popped open, spilling the unused film. I stopped around a corner of the house, peeking back long enough to catch the license plate on the white BMW: "GRGORY." The windows were shaded; I couldn't see who was inside.

My sore knee forced me into a stiff-legged skip as I raced across the short lawn on the lake side of the house and out onto the dry margin of the lakebed. I stuck close to the lakeshore, my eyes nearly blind from sweat and the glare of the midday sun. Two houses down I crossed a lawn of straw-colored grass and hobbled up the dirt track that led back to the blacktop road.

I came out a hundred yards beyond the bushes where I'd hidden the truck. No sign of Gregory's BMW. I drove along the blacktop road in the other direction until I found a way back out to Tumble Lake Road, where I stopped at a bait shop for a quart of soda.

As I drove, steering wheel in one hand and Dr. Pepper in the other, I reminded myself that none of the tools had my name on them and I was almost certain that no one had seen me. If only I'd gotten some photos, something I could show to Ramirez. The paintings in the shed were what I needed, something that tied Washburn to a criminal enterprise and maybe a reason for his murder.

I wiped the sweat out of my eyes and thought of Gwen. All I knew for certain was that she knew something was in the shed. I didn't want to drag her into something unless I was sure she was involved. I also didn't want her to know I'd been following her unless I absolutely had to. For some reason I still cared what she thought of me.

Hope is the dandelion of the human heart.

I stopped at the apartment for a quick shower and change, then drove to the Longhorn. The bar was empty, except for Walter and two of his ex-Marine buddies, Frank and Rick.

"Howdy, boys," I greeted, as I limped over to a barstool.

"Stu," said Walter. "Got a couple of things for you. I don't exactly know how either got here. First was left on the bar when I was in the men's room. Second turned up while I was bringing some beer up from the cellar."

Walter handed me a sheet of paper with a pencil sketch of me standing behind the bar, my sleeves rolled up, a bottle of beer in each hand. A note paper-clipped to the sketch read, "Daniel asked me to give this to you. Chris."

I passed it to Frank and Rick, who praised it for actually looking like me.

Walter reached behind the cash register and pulled out a sealed white envelope with my name on it written in a flowing, elegant hand. "I found this leaning against the beer tap."

I opened the flap. It was a card, with a photograph of rumpled white sheets on a bed.

"Stu. I owe you another apology. I'll stop by tonight. Gwen."

I slid the card into my pocket, not sure whether to be excited or wary.

I was filling a pitcher of beer for a group of nurses who had just gotten off an early shift at the Med Center when Gwen pushed through the door and propped her sunglasses on the top of her head. I nodded to her and delivered the pitcher. When I returned, she was perched on one of the stools, her shoulder bag next to her on the bar. I slipped a napkin in front of her.

"Mrs. Washburn," I said, setting a bourbon-with-ice in front of her. She accepted the drink without taking her eye off me. She seemed both worried and uncertain. That made two of us.

"Please, call me Gwen."

"Okay, Gwen. I want to apologize for bothering you yesterday."

"No, I should apologize. I overreacted when you came to the house, calling the police. Seeing you made me nervous."

I started to speak, but she stopped me by briefly squeezing my hand. It was all I could do to let go.

"Nervous isn't a bad thing," she said. "I just don't know how to react, given everything that's happened."

"I understand," I replied, not sure what I understood. I looked at my watch. Five to five. I opened a Shiner and slid it in front of the empty stool at the end of the bar.

"Invisible drinker?" she asked.

"It's for Harry. He'll be here soon."

On cue, Harry Clintock walked in, his bear-like body rocking from side to side as he crossed to his stool four down from Gwen's.

"Harry, Gwen," I said. "Gwen, Harry."

"Hello, Harry," Gwen greeted.

Harry lifted his bottle in reply.

I walked down his way. "You doing all right?" I asked as I stacked some napkins.

He nodded and motioned toward Gwen with his eyes. "I've Just Seen a Face?" he asked in a soft voice so she wouldn't hear.

I shrugged, not able to think of a song that conveyed my mix of caution and desire.

"Big man," Gwen observed when I returned.

"He's our unofficial bouncer. Same stool every night. Four beers: one at five, seven, nine, and eleven. He likes to have everything in order. Not real keen on making decisions."

"What did he say about me?"

"What makes you think he was talking about you?"

"I learned in grade school how to tell when the boys were talking about the girls."

I nodded, conceding the point. "He said you seem nice."

"What did you say?"

"Do you really want to know?"

"No." She smiled, sets of fine lines radiating from good and bad eye alike. I could look at this face for a long time, I thought.

The door to the Longhorn burst open and a crew of eight or ten from the City Works Division walked in, followed by half a dozen from the Journalism Department at the university. Pauline called out their orders. I put up two pitchers for the beer drinkers, then began assembling a round of margaritas. By the time I finished, the worried, almost anxious look had returned to Gwen's face.

"Is everything okay?" I asked.

"I'm a bit embarrassed. I have a favor to ask. Please feel free to say no."

I held up my hands in my best go-for-it gesture. I couldn't imagine a favor I wouldn't do for her.

"I'd like you to escort me to the opening of the ArtFest exhibition," she said. "I'm taking Andrew's place as a judge and I'd rather not be there alone."

She misinterpreted my surprised reaction. "Your friend," she said, nodding toward Pauline, "told me you used to be a minister. If you're worried, I'll introduce you as Reverend Carlson. All very appropriate. And in return I'll make you dinner."

At that moment Chris appeared behind Gwen, giving me a questioning look that she couldn't see.

"Howdy, Gwen," he said, climbing onto the next stool.

"Hello, Chris," she said coolly.

"I hope I'm not interrupting anything," Chris said.

"No," I replied. "We were just talking about the ArtFest exhibition."

Gwen looked at her watch. "I have to get going. The insurance agent is meeting me at Andrew's cottage on Tumble Lake. Someone set fire to a small utility building. Probably some kids. Chris, it was nice seeing you again," she said. She handed me a printed card. "Here's the invitation for the opening. I have to go earlier. I'll meet you there."

"Can I bring anything?"

"You bring the wine."

"White or red?"

"Red. I'll cook Italian."

"I'll be there." We shook hands and she left. I hadn't actually said yes; she'd assumed I wouldn't turn her down and she was right. I handed Chris a cold Shiner and a bottle of Tabasco.

"Did you get that drawing from Daniel?" he asked.

"Got it," I said, pointing behind the bar to where Walter had taped the sketch. "Thanks."

"I did a supply run to Jenkin's Art House after visiting Daniel. Thought I'd drop it off." Chris looked back at the door where Gwen had just exited. "I didn't know you two knew each other."

"I actually met her a while ago," I said, not sure how much of the truth to make public.

"Didn't seem too happy to see me," he said, shaking the Tabasco in his beer.

"She's replacing her husband as a judge for the exhibition. Maybe she feels awkward being around one of the artists."

"No, shit. On the panel? I should kiss her feet." He pointed to the invitation for the opening. "I was going to offer you one of those."

"She asked me to escort her to the opening," I said, quickly slipping the invitation into my pocket along with her note and adding, "in my capacity as retired clergy."

"Yeah, Daniel tells me his mom thinks you're his minister."

Between customers I gave Chris a description of Daniel's mother's visit to the Longhorn. After he left, I had a chance to pull out Gwen's note and the Artfest invitation. Had I needed proof of Gwen's innocence, the burning of the shed supplied it. Gregory obviously torched the place when he discovered someone had found the paintings.

I pictured sitting across from Gwen in her freshly painted, royal blue dining room. I knew enough about grieving to avoid involvement where the intensity has nothing to do with me or sex and everything to do with a wound only time will heal. For both of our sakes, I reminded myself, we'll be just friends.

Chapter ★ Twenty-One

I basked in the afterglow of Gwen's attention until John Springer arrived. He was wearing khaki shorts and a blue polo shirt. John's the only person I know who has his causal clothes laundered and starched.

"Let me ask you one thing," I said, handing him his usual scotch-and-soda. "Did you tell Jocelyn where I was working?"

"Nice to see you, too, Stuart. No, I didn't tell Jocelyn. She did, however, stop by to find out why you're ignoring her. I said you were a busy man. I also told her I'd asked you to preach for me."

"What did she say?"

"She said she didn't think you'd do it. I, however, declared my faith in you."

"You can be a real bastard."

John smiled and raised his glass. "Only to my friends. Professionally I'm all sweetness and light.

"The request still stands," he added. "I'd love to have you preach in August."

I grunted and went off to check on the customers along the bar. When I returned John was gone, having left a ten-dollar bill and a business card. I picked up the card: Jocelyn Wendell Graham, Assistant Minister, Community Christian Church.

I shoved the change from John's bill into the tip jar and Jocelyn's card into the trash.

I had to admire John. If anything would drive me to preach again, it was Jocelyn believing that I wouldn't or couldn't do it. Preaching was the one thing I did better than her and we both knew it, although she rarely admitted it. Her preaching was always preachy, full of righteous sentiment. No doubt, no struggle, no good news. John's persistence was his way of saying that he knew it, too. It had been a couple of years since anyone said to me, "Good sermon." I had to laugh. John was applying pressure with surgical precision.

I was still laughing at myself two hours later when the telephone rang. I had just given last call to the handful of customers remaining in the bar.

It had to be Jocelyn and I had no one to cover for me. I took a deep breath and picked up the handset.

"Longhorn Lounge."

"Stu Carlson?" a male voice asked. It sounded flat and very serious.

"Speaking."

"I have a message for a friend of yours named Blaine Waters. Tell him he could lose his passport if he doesn't mind his own business. He'll understand."

The line went dead. I stared at the receiver and slowly hung up. Oh, shit. Gregory had recognized me and figured where I worked, probably where I lived. So that's who smashed the windows on the truck and stole my camera.

And there wasn't a damned thing I could do about it. Thoughts crowded my head as I began washing dirty glasses, my hands on autopilot. The police weren't going to arrest Gregory because I think he threatened me. I had no proof, no real evidence. I could hide, move out of my apartment, take off a few days from work. That wouldn't help. I didn't know how much Gregory knew about me. If I was being followed, he could track me down wherever I went. He might have been calling from his BMW outside in the alley.

Goddamn it! I shoved a dirty wineglass into the soapy water. The stem snapped off against the bottom of the sink. When I pulled my hand out of the water there was a ragged gash at the base of my thumb. I rinsed the wound, patted it dry, and inspected it for bits of glass. The cut seemed clean, so I pulled out the first aid kit. My anger leached away as I applied disinfectant and a bandage, leaving me drained and tired.

I had to rouse myself to say goodnight to the last customers. I skipped a post-work drink and closed up quickly. After locking the front door and dimming the lights, I borrowed the flashlight Brownie kept above the fuse box in the back hall. I poked my head out the fire door and swung the beam along the alley walls. The dumpster, a stack of empty liquor boxes, some garbage cans behind the shoe repair shop next door, cracked pavement, rough brick walls. No movement, no figures in the shadows, no sudden glare of headlights. Just the alley. I slipped out the fire door and turned to make sure the lock had latched.

"I am the gut that pukes the wisdom of the Lord!" screamed a voice in my ear as a hand descended on my shoulder.

I whirled around, swinging the flashlight as hard as I could. It connected with a sickening thwack against the side of someone's head, then flew from my hand.

Bob, the alley prophet, staggered back a few steps, his hands on the side of his face, his eyes wide and wild. In the dim, bluish glow from the streetlight at the end of the alley, blood dripped black through the stubble of his unshaven cheek.

"What are you doing?" I shouted, my heart hammering on my ribs, my mind racing to catch up with my actions.

Bob let out a low moan and squeezed his eyes tight. Over the next few seconds, the instant strength in my limbs melted away. "Don't surprise me like that," I blurted out. Tears blurred my vision. "I could have really hurt you."

I took a step in his direction. The moan increased in pitch, as if he could see me approaching, then turned into a high wail that stopped me where I stood. Abruptly he stopped and opened his eyes.

"The blood of the lamb," he whimpered. "The blood of the ox." Without another word he sprinted toward the nearest end of the alley. I hobbled after him, but by the time I reached the street, he was gone.

The threatening phone call and Bob's screams locked together in my head. I've got to do something.

Got to find him. I might have killed him. Someone might kill me.

I retrieved the flashlight, locked the rear door of the Longhorn, and limped around to where I'd parked the pickup.

Chapter ★ Twenty-Two

For the next hour I cruised the streets looking for Bob and checking the rearview mirror. No white BMWs, only the occasional pickup or jacked-up muscle car. The final place to look was River Park. I pulled into a parking lot and scanned the baseball diamonds and picnic areas, all lit by a hazy moon a few days from full. No Bob. I gave up.

I keep a fifth of Jack Daniels, usually untouched, in my glove compartment. For emergencies. I took a long pull from the bottle while I was still in the truck, three or four more while I walked across center field in the direction of the levy.

I lay down on the stubby fingers of Johnson grass covering the gentle slope to the river. The water looked like a sheet of tan plastic, with only the illusion of movement. Ten feet out, the handle of a shopping cart stuck into the air. The levy stretched for a quarter mile in either direction and empty ball fields covered my back; I could easily see anyone coming.

For a while I paid attention only to the smoky bite of the whiskey and the motionless blanket of warm air on top of me. A crowd of thoughts was knocking on my door, but I pretended I wasn't home. After a few minutes, or many minutes, I crawled to the river. The water was as cool as the breeze we hadn't had in weeks. I took another drink, then two, and stripped off my clothes.

Mud oozed between my toes. I flopped forward, arms wide, then rolled over on my back, a great, pale whale in the moonlight. The current pulled me slowly toward the Gulf of Mexico. I anchored my foot to the handle of the grocery cart. My thoughts finally let themselves in, all shouts and elbows in a phone booth.

Gregory's trying to scare me, hurt me, and it's working. I could have killed Bob. I cut myself and made him bleed.

Daniel's in jail for now, forever, and having a great time, goddamn him.

Andrew Washburn dies in my hands. On my lips. I don't know what to feel. Nothing at all.

I spend my time pawing through his widow's garbage. Following her all over the county like a goddamn stalker.

Jocelyn's closing in. I have to get away. Can't go backwards. The same mistakes again and again and again.

I can't preach. Nothing to say. I failed. Fucked up. For good.

I stood up in the waist-deep water.

"What the hell do you want?" I screamed at the sky or the moon or the heavens. "Leave me alone!"

The reply was swift. Everything around me suddenly burst into light. The water drops on my pale skin sparkled like sequins.

"This is the police," said an amplified voice behind the spotlight. "Get out of the river."

The world was backwards. I shielded my eyes and looked for my clothes on the bank near the light. Slowly the realization formed in my head. The police were on the opposite side, by the warehouses across the river from the park. I turned around and waded for the bank. The spotlight followed me out of the water.

I scrambled up the slope, clutching my clothes to my bare and dripping chest, and hobbled across the grass to my pickup. I managed to pull on my shoes before driving slowly and deliberately out of the park. No police car showed up to stop me; a drunk in the river wasn't worth the effort.

Outside my apartment, I pulled on my shoes and inspected the dark stairs with the flashlight before getting out. The alcohol roaring through my blood made each act a complex and distant process. On the landing I went down on my knees to examine the lock for any signs of tampering. My clothes spent the night where I dropped them on the stairs. I searched all four rooms, then locked myself in and set Shadrach, Meshach, and Abednego in a line between the front door and the door to the bedroom. I even looked under the bed.

I swallowed three or four aspirin and drank a pint of water before collapsing on the bed.

Chapter ★ Twenty-Three

My first thought was that I was wearing shoes without socks. I raised my head to view the length of my body. I wasn't wearing anything else. I started to sit up, only to be slammed back down by a spear through the brain. The events of the previous evening came back to me—the threatening call, my gashed thumb, the attack on Bob, the bourbon by in the river—along with a collapsible stomach and a tongue the size of the Goodyear blimp. I hadn't been this hung over since the months after I walked out on Jocelyn.

I slowly pulled the telephone over to the bed. On my third attempt I reached the Union Gospel Mission, one of the shelters where Bob slept and took meals. Brother Roger, the rail-thin Pentecostal who ran the place, answered the phone. From previous encounters I knew he viewed bartenders as travel agents for the devil; I identified myself as a small business owner concerned for the homeless man who frequented my alley. To my relief, Bob had shown up for breakfast and the obligatory bible study with only a small cut on the side of his head. Brother Roger invited me to his Wednesday Businessman's Prayer Breakfast. I mumbled an excuse and silently vowed to send the Mission a donation.

By this time I remembered it was Friday. I'd promised to visit Daniel. I dialed the jail and scheduled a time after lunch.

My body craved coffee, but my conscience demanded penance. I forced myself out of bed, into shorts, and out the door for a run. I had to wear sunglasses to keep the sun from drilling holes through my eyes. For the first mile my head and gut reverberated with each step. After that the world was too hot and hazy for me think about anything else. My course took me through the park, along the levy. I spotted the grocery cart, breaking the chocolate-colored water into slow-motion swirls. The bottle of Jack Daniels had disappeared.

The run had its desired effect. I sat on the landing outside my apartment, more empty than sick. Once inside, I downed a quart of orange juice while the coffee brewed. Given my still delicate condition, I opted to brunch on a stack of dry toast.

When I walked into the visiting room at the jail, it was clear Daniel was in a better mood and had a hell of lot more energy than me. He carried a sheaf of drawings, which he then held up to the glass, one by one. The drawings were good, very good, mostly portraits in colored pencil of the guards and other prisoners, along with a small rendering of the view from the roof of the jail. I thanked him for the sketch Chris had delivered to the Longhorn.

As the visit drew to a close, I again felt the resentment that Daniel had found a way to flourish in a small cell. Only his request that I visit again on Monday and his declaration that the visits meant a lot to him kept me from a round of misplaced anger and self-pity.

I sat in the cab of my pickup, accepting the fact that there was nothing more I could do for Daniel; probably never was. Which left me two hours until work. I could sit in the jailhouse parking lot and slow bake my brain. Or blow ten bucks over the indoor batting cages on Old Forth Worth Highway.

Or I could confess my sins to Gwen. Tell her everything: my conversation with Wendy Green, the trip to Dallas, the break-in at the lake house, everything. I wanted it all in the open. I didn't have the strength to hide or dissemble.

I drove toward Pecan Creek.

As I turned onto Gwen's block, she emerged from the townhouse, wearing a dark dress, wide-brimmed straw hat, and sunglasses. I eased over to the curb and watched as she backed out the Mercedes. I let her get two blocks ahead, then followed. After a few turns we headed west on Jarvis, then right on Van Buren, toward the river and not Tumble Lake. A mile further she pulled into Brazos Hills, a cemetery on a bluff overlooking the West Branch.

I parked near the entrance and climbed out. A few ancient oak trees shaded this older section of the cemetery. The monuments stood tall and erect, a collection of slabs and obelisks and angels. Out beyond the trees, newer grave markers, low to the ground and of a uniform size, dotted the lawn like rows of stitches in the unnaturally green grass. A trickle of cars rolled slowly along the road. A few individuals searched among the graves, heads bent down to read the names on the markers.

I sat on a stone bench under the last tree and watched Gwen get out of her car. She walked up a small hillside with a wrapped florist's package under her arm to where a new grave was outlined in brown, the edges of sod burnt by the sun. She stood for a moment, then drew half a dozen cut lilies from the package and laid them across the marker. She stood, motionless, for another minute before returning to her car and driving away.

I remained on the bench. Gwen didn't need my uninvited confession, not now, not ever. I leaned back against the tree, eyes closed, and pictured the cemetery outside of Bloom, the small town where I'd had my church. The cemetery was a patch of rocky soil on the state highway. The VFW painted the iron gate white once a year, and the four churches in town took turns chopping the weeds and sparse grass. My first funeral, two weeks after I started at the church, was on a day like this, with a burning sun and the ground as hard as fired clay. Warren Johnson had died of a heart attack while loading sacks of concrete onto his truck at the Farm and Road store. No one liked him much —he had a reputation for shooting any animal that wandered across his property on the edge of town—yet everyone turned out, for both the service and the graveside.

For the second time in a week, I became aware of Death beside me, only now as a searing, cleansing light that scoured the granite of the bench and stripped the shadows from the tombstones. I knew it wasn't there for me, that it was only visiting. We sat together, then I was alone.

I shielded my eyes against the glaring sun to look up the hillside at the clutch of lilies draped over Washburn's grave marker. Whatever else I thought of Washburn, I was glad Gwen made the effort.

CHAPTER ★ TWENTY-FOUR

I arrived at the Longhorn drained, yet relaxed, as if I'd had every muscle kneaded by a professional. Maybe Death had shown up to take back the ghost of Andrew Washburn and give me peace. Or maybe I'd simply reached my limit; too many threats, too much hot weather. Either way it came to the same thing: I was determined to be what I was and should have stayed, the big guy behind the bar who serves you a beer, listens to your story, and cleans up after you leave. Daniel's lawyer could get him out of jail. I'd escort Gwen to the opening, say goodnight, and save myself for a woman who didn't see half as much with two good eyes. John Springer would have to find a real preacher. And when I finally ran into Jocelyn, I'd say whatever came into my head.

Walter had another note for me. I recognized Jocelyn's handwriting, neat lines of printed letters. I flipped it into the garbage and asked Walter to swap shifts with me the next day. I'd work the afternoon, he'd take over at five o'clock, and I'd have time to shower and change for the opening.

The evening was busy and uneventful. The Possum Kingdom Ramblers played two sets of blue grass, the double mandolins bouncing off the ceiling. Harry helped me toss out a drunk who tried to make his point with a beer mug. I earned a five-dollar tip by reciting Lou Gehrig's farewell speech from The Pride of the Yankees: "Some people say I've had a bad break, but I consider myself to be the luckiest man on the face the earth."

Four hours later I had the Longhorn to myself. I finished wiping down the bar, then pulled out the bottle of Laphroig and a brandy snifter. If I was no longer haunted by Andrew Washburn's death, I could return to my single malt scotch. I held the bottle up to the light and swirled the four inches of dark amber liquid up the clear glass sides. I uncapped the bottle and tipped its neck toward the glass.

Something wasn't right.

I stared at the bottle in my hand. The label on the fifth of Laphroig I had been slowly emptying over the last three months had a scrunched, upper left-hand corner just above the red letter "L". This label was smooth from top to bottom.

I poured a little of the whiskey in the glass and brought it up to my nose. The strong, peaty odor of the liquor filled my head. Behind it I thought—or imagined—I picked up a faint smell of bitter almonds.

I emptied the glass in the sink, carefully washed it, then decided to throw it in the trash. I capped the bottle, washed my hands, and sat at the bar. I thought about calling Ramirez. And say what? "I found another bottle of booze full of cyanide. Could you test it for me?" I felt the tension flow back into my shoulders and neck as I imagined Ramirez's damning appraisal when I tried to explain why a sleazy art dealer from Dallas had gone to the trouble of poisoning a nobody bartender in Travis City.

I decided to call Cheryl Lester and see if she could have the whiskey tested at the hospital. If it were poisoned, then I'd call the police. It was already two a.m. I resisted the temptation to wake her up and instead packed the bottle in an empty plastic garbage sack.

I went out through the alley, holding the sack as if it were a leaky biohazard bag. The only other vehicles I saw on the trip home were a police patrol car on Jarvis and station wagon full of drunken high school boys. Back at my apartment, I left the bag on the small table by the front door.

I took a beer out of the refrigerator, too wound up to sleep. The top showed no signs of tampering, so I opened it and sat at the top of the stairs, looking down at the pickup. A yellow glow from the sodium lamp at the end of the alley turned the faded, blue paint into the green of old copper and filled the cab with deep shadows. My mind started turning over the how's and who's. I shut off the thoughts as best I could. There'd be time enough for that after I found out what was in the whiskey bottle.

I went back inside, dreading the idea of lying in bed and not sleeping. I turned on the television and slumped in the easy chair, remote control in hand. *Mary Tyler Moore*, the *Ghost and Mr. Chicken*, Australian Rules Football. At some point I fell asleep.

CHAPTER ★ TWENTY-FIVE

I stumbled into the kitchen five hours later as if getting off a two-day bus from L.A. I talked to myself for a minute to make sure my voice was working, then hunted for Cheryl and Rusty's number on the doodle-infested paper taped to the wall by the telephone. Their machine answered. I tried the main switchboard number at the Med Center next. The operator took my number. I told her it was urgent, but not an emergency.

Cheryl called back within five minutes.

"This is Dr. Lester returning your call."

"Cheryl, this is Stu. I think someone tried to poison me last night."

"I'll send an ambulance—"

"Don't worry. I didn't swallow it. It was in a bottle of scotch. I think it's cyanide. I wanted to know if you could get it tested for me."

"If there's any chance it contains cyanide, take it to the police."

"I don't want to go to them unless I'm sure. They're already on my case for talking to people about the murder at the reception last week."

Cheryl was silent.

"I promise I'll go straight to the police if there's cyanide in the whiskey," I added.

"I shouldn't do this," she muttered. "I have a break at ten. Meet me outside the resident's lounge, second floor, North Building."

That left me an hour and a half. After a shower, a pot of coffee, and a stack of jelly toast I felt almost ready for almost anything.

The Med Center sprawls over the remnants of the old German business district. The original two-story, red brick building of Travis City Hospital is dwarfed by its numerous and larger offspring, boxes sheathed in matching red brick and circled by bands of reflecting glass.

I found a spot in the shade on the lower deck of the parking garage and crossed over the street on a covered walkway, the bottle of scotch occasionally bumping into my leg from inside the plastic sack. I checked a map and set off through a maze of carpeted tunnels and hallways, following a blue stripe near the ceiling that promised to convey me to the North Building. I found the resident's lounge at the far end of a general ward on the second floor. It was a square room with a rust colored sofa and a few armchairs that were modern before I was born. A bearded young man in a white coat stood at a counter, stirring a cup of coffee. Another resident slept on the sofa, huddled in a fetal position, his back to the room.

"I'm looking for Cheryl Lester," I announced.

The standing man consulted his watch without turning around. "She should be here by now. Must be held up with rounds. Have a seat."

I sat in one of the chairs and started thumbing through a magazine filled with incomprehensible articles and glowing drug advertisements. Cheryl arrived a few minutes later.

"Sorry to keep you waiting," she said briskly. "Is that the specimen?"

I held up the bag. "This is it."

"Follow me."

We rode the elevator to the basement. Cheryl didn't say anything. I took her silence as anger at me for asking and herself for agreeing. The long underground hallway was lined with large pieces of lab equipment, some still in packing crates. We stopped outside a door marked "Chemistry."

"Give me the bag. Wait out here."

Through the window I could see Cheryl talking to a young man in blue jeans, T-shirt, and a white lab coat. At one point the technician looked at me and grinned.

Cheryl returned to the hallway. "It will only take a minute. It's a relatively quick test."

I nodded. My palms were sweaty, despite the near-freezing air-conditioning in the hospital.

"Does this have anything to do with the poisoning at the reception?" she asked.

"I don't know."

"What makes you think there's cyanide in the whiskey?"

"The label on the bottle. It was torn. Now all of sudden it's smooth. And I think I smelled bitter almonds."

"A good thing you did," the technician said from the doorway. "I can't give you an exact concentration, but there's probably enough cyanide in that bottle to stop an elephant. A sip or two would have rung your number."

"Thanks, Jerry," Cheryl said.

"Anytime. You want the bottle back?"

"Why don't you keep it here until the police call for it."

Jerry nodded and disappeared back into his lab.

Cheryl escorted me to a telephone and watched while I left a message for Ramirez, asking him to meet me at the Longhorn. I also called Walter, who was setting up for the day, and told him not to open until I got there.

At the front entrance to the Med Center, Cheryl gave me a wordless hug before disappearing back into the building.

Chapter ★ Twenty-Six

It was a few minutes before eleven when I arrived at the Longhorn. The closed sign still hung on the door. Inside, Ramirez and Drainer were sitting at a table with Brownie, the owner, and Walter.

"What the hell's all this bullshit about poison?" Brownie asked as she let out a cloud of smoke. Ramirez leaned back to avoid the fumes, while Drainer stuck his nose in their direction, the reflex of an ex-smoker.

"Please, let us ask the questions," said Ramirez.

Brownie scowled and put a wall of smoke between herself and the detective.

"Your message said a bottle of liquor had cyanide in it," Ramirez said to me.

"That's right. One of the scotches." I pointed at the back bar. "Called Laphroig."

"Where is the bottle now?"

"At the Med Center chemistry lab. I asked someone

there to test it for me. When they told me it contained cyanide, I called you."

Ramirez glanced at Drainer, who heaved himself out of his chair and walked over to the telephone on the bar.

"What made you think the bottle was poisoned?"

"The label was smooth instead of crinkled. And when I sniffed it, I thought I smelled bitter almonds."

"Why did you leave with the bottle instead of calling the police?"

"I couldn't believe that the bottle had been poisoned. I figured there must be some other explanation, so I thought I'd check it out myself."

Ramirez stared at me for a few seconds.

"He's right about the whiskey," Drainer called out from behind the bar. "Cyanide. A shitload."

"Call Forensics," Ramirez replied. "I want standard crime scene and a portable lab." He turned to face Brownie. "I'm afraid, Mrs. Brown, we're going to have to keep your establishment closed until we can go over it for evidence and ensure that no other bottles or foodstuffs have been tampered with."

"What the hell . . ." Brownie didn't finish her sentence. She bent over the table and burst into a fit of hacking coughs.

Walter stepped in. "How long will we be closed?"

"One hour, maybe two."

"Can you at least use the alley?" Brownie asked, her voice sounding as if it had been scraped off a cast iron skillet. "People see a bunch of goddamn police cars sitting out front and a closed sign on the door in the middle of the day, it scares them away. I spent twenty years building up the reputation of this place."

"We will be as discreet as possible." With Brownie, a local business owner, Ramirez was all public affairs. He called over to Drainer. "Have the crime scene team and lab van park in the alley." He turned toward the table. "I need to speak to Mr. Carlson alone."

Walter hesitated, then walked toward the bar. Brownie blew of a jet of cigarette smoke in my direction and followed Walter.

"I must ask you not to leave," Ramirez announced, "and not to touch anything behind the bar." Brownie grunted and joined Walter in a booth. Ramirez turned toward me. "Tell me again what happened."

"It's like I said. I was pouring myself a drink after closing up last night, when I noticed that the label wasn't torn like before."

"Describe the label on any other bottle."

I tried to look over toward the bar. Ramirez's hand shot up and blocked my view, stopping within an inch of slapping my face.

"Without looking, Mr. Carlson."

"I think the label on the Highland Park is tilted a little, as if it was glued on by hand."

Ramirez looked at Drainer, who was listening from behind the bar. Drainer checked the bottles and nodded back to Ramirez.

"Why didn't you call us immediately?"

"I didn't want to believe it was poisoned. And I didn't want to call you up and cry 'Cyanide,' then have it be a false alarm. After you warned me not to interfere with the investigation, I figured you'd take it as a trick to get Daniel Lackland out of jail."

Ramirez stared at me for a moment and then wrote something in his notebook.

"You said you smelled cyanide?" he asked.

"I thought so, but it's hard to tell. The scotch has a strong, smoky odor."

"You know what cyanide smells like?"

"After trying to revive Washburn I don't think I'll ever forget."

He nodded. At least I scored one point.

A noise came from the back hallway. Ramirez excused himself and went to give instructions to the forensics team. Two men and a woman in white jumpers with "POLICE FORENSICS" stenciled on the back brought in several large cases of equipment. One of the technicians began taking pictures of the bar while the others unpacked an assortment of tubes and bottles.

"We would like to search your apartment," Ramirez said as he sat down again.

"You think I put the cyanide in the bottle myself, don't you?"

"What would you think, Mr. Carlson?"

His reasoning was sound and we both knew it. I wasn't exactly comfortable with Ramirez opening my drawers and lifting my rugs, but I had nothing to hide, no reason to act tough.

"With your permission we can save the city the expense of securing a search warrant. In fact, I would like to go there when we finish here."

Before I could explain that I was scheduled to work that afternoon, someone rapped on the door. Rusty pressed his face to the glass, trying to peer into the bar.

"It's Rusty Martin," I said, "the other nighttime

bartender."

Ramirez nodded to Drainer, who unlocked the door.

"Stu, Cheryl told me what happened. I'll cover for you this afternoon. You get some rest."

I thanked him before Drainer could usher him to the booth with the others.

"I guess you can search anytime," I said to Ramirez.

"When was the last time you used the bottle?" continued Ramirez.

"At least two weeks ago, before the reception. I'm about the only person who drinks from it."

"Was it among the bottles you took to the reception?"

"No."

"Who knows you are the primary user?"

"A lot of people. I like the single malts and I'm not shy about telling folks." I pictured Gwen sitting at the bar. "Which bottles?" she had asked.

"Anyone you told recently?"

"No, not that I can remember."

"Who had access to the bottle?"

"Anyone behind the bar or sitting on the end stool could reach it. But it wouldn't have happened at night. Harry Clintock, our bouncer, sits there every night, five to midnight. You'd have to ask Walter about the day shift."

"Can you think of any reason why someone would want to poison you?"

I was ready to tell Ramirez everything I'd found out, or thought I'd found out, except about the paintings in the shed. I couldn't explain my visits to the lake house without implicating Gwen.

"There might be a reason. Earlier this week I talked

with some people about Washburn's murder."

"Go on."

"I went to see Daniel at the jail because he's a friend, and I stopped to see his lawyer because I told Daniel I'd talk to her. Then at the funeral Wendy Green introduced herself. We talked and she mentioned that Washburn had some art dealing with a gallery in Dallas named M. Gregory. I stopped in the gallery and discovered they're selling counterfeit works of art."

"How did you find that out?"

"I pretended to be dumb and rich. They showed a bronze sculpture by Remington that turns out to a notorious fake."

"Anything else?"

"Gregory or someone who works for him threatened me over the telephone on Tuesday night." I decided not to mention the busted windows of my pickup. I didn't want to give Ramirez another reason to ask me why I hadn't called the police.

"This was not important enough to report to the police?"

I shrugged. I only later realized that he was more alarmed at my carelessness than angry at my withholding information.

Ramirez flipped through the pages of his notebook. "Is there anything else you want to tell me, Mr. Carlson?"

"Not that I can think of. You still want to check my apartment?"

"Very much." He stood up, signaling the end of the interview.

I walked over to the booth where Rusty, Walter, and Brownie were sitting. Brownie got up without a word and exited through the doorway into the kitchen; I'd have to spend weeks, maybe months, repairing that relationship. I asked Walter and Rusty about the customers the previous day; they hadn't seen anyone who resembled Gregory or Warren, the security guard at the gallery. Neither of them pushed me to explain what was going on.

By twelve thirty the forensics team had failed to find any more cyanide and Ramirez had finished questioning Brownie and my fellow employees. The Longhorn opened for business and the police escorted me to my apartment.

Ramirez climbed the stairs with me, Drainer puffing behind. A handwritten message was taped to the door, each letter precisely shaped. I tore off the paper with an angry swipe. Jocelyn had tracked me to the door of my apartment, which was about to be invaded by strangers.

"You want to read this, too?" I asked, shoving the note at Ramirez.

Before I could regret the action, Ramirez scanned the page.

"I believe this is personal." He handed me back the note. I shoved it into my pocket, unread.

They searched quietly and efficiently, while I sat in the overstuffed chair. One of the technicians set up a collection of test tubes and chemicals on the small kitchen table next to my chrome plated toaster and duck shaped salt and pepper shakers.

Fifteen minutes later the technician walked out of the kitchen. "I tried to put the caps back on the beer," he said. I thanked him and held open the door as he carried the black equipment case out to the unmarked car.

As if on cue, Drainer walked out of the bathroom and

Ramirez appeared at the doorway to the kitchen.

"Thank you for your cooperation, Mr. Carlson," Ramirez said.

"I assume you didn't find any bottles of cyanide?"

"No." Ramirez might as well have been wearing sunglasses, for all the expression I could read in his eyes.

"Let us know immediately if you see or hear anything suspicious," he continued. "We do not take attempted murder lightly."

"Can we keep this from getting public?" I asked. "I'm thinking about Brownie and the Longhorn."

"I have no reason to make a public statement. Should criminal charges be filed, that would be a different matter."

I held the door open again, ever the host. Ramirez stopped at a table by the door, where I'd left the volume of Jonathan Edwards' sermons a week earlier.

"I find Edwards melodramatic," he said, tapping the cover. "But I appreciate his stark depiction of the judgment that awaits us. It makes my job easier."

He looked back at me from the landing. "I hope you find something to make your job easier, Mr. Carlson."

I would have been happier if Ramirez had arrested me for obstructing justice, instead of consigning me to a higher judgment. I closed the door and pulled out the note from Jocelyn, caught the phrase, "beyond anger to reconciliation," and stuffed it in the trash.

I walked around the apartment, returning my toothbrush to the holder over the sink in the bathroom, repositioning the photographs on top of the dresser in the bedroom, and putting the mayonnaise back on the shelf of the refrigerator door in the kitchen. I tried not to think about what conclusions Ramirez drew from my personal effects.

I was still reclaiming my space when Chris called. I didn't have the energy to tell him what had happened.

"You're meeting Gwen at the reception, right?" he asked.

"That's right."

"I need a favor. My car broke down this afternoon and nobody'll look at it until Monday. If I can get to the opening, I can always find a ride from there."

"Sure. I'll pick you up about six."

I hung up, set the alarm, and fell on the bed.

I slept without dreaming and woke three hours later, more rested than I'd felt since Andrew Washburn's death. With the police after Gregory, I told myself as I stood under the shower, everything is behind me and I can get my life back.

Chapter ★ Twenty-Seven

I stopped at Sternwood's Liquor Warehouse to buy wine for dinner. A California Pinot Noir with an interesting label. I checked my reflection in the "Hey You, Have a Brew" mirror behind the cashier: black dinner jacket, black velvet cummerbund, and black pants with a midnight blue silk stripe down the outer seam of the leg—standard items in the wardrobe of a bartender with an eye for going-out-of-business sales at formal wear stores. The occasion being an art opening in the heart of Texas, I'd selected my state flag bow tie, white star on a blue field on the left, red and white stripe on the right. I might not be handsome, but I get noticed.

Chris emerged from the shadows of the entryway as I pulled up to the old Texas Sun factory. He wore straight leg black jeans and a black T-shirt, topped by an electric blue tuxedo jacket with black satin lapels. He dropped a black canvas bag on the floor of the pickup as he pulled himself into the seat.

"Nice jacket," I said.

"Thanks. Nice tie."

"Remember the Alamo." I swung the pickup around at the dead end and headed west. "Going on a trip?"

"Sangria for a party after the opening. Want some?"

"No, thanks."

At the traffic light at Santa Clara and River Park, I wiped the sweat off my forehead with a handkerchief. The temperature seemed to have dropped a few degrees, though it might have been my imagination.

"Is Daniel's painting still in the exhibition?" I asked.

"Delivered it myself when I brought mine over."

The opening was at the Winters Art Museum, a set of giant concrete cubes piled up like children's blocks in a grove of trees at the east end of River Park. The carelessness of the arrangement was deceptive; the cubes surrounded a well-shaded atrium and were positioned to provide maximum natural light for the galleries. The few shaded parking spaces were already taken. Seven o'clock and the sun was still a blowtorch.

"You better bring your wine in," I said, holding up the paper bag with my bottle. "It'll cook out here."

We stowed our gear behind one of the coat racks in the reception area, then handed in our invitations at the entrance to the main gallery.

"I'll catch you later," said Chris. "Thanks for the ride."

"Anytime."

A hundred and fifty people were spread through the L-shaped gallery, talking in knots of three and four or slowly moving from work to work, filling the space with a pleasant hum of voices, shuffling feet, and clinking glasses. Two bars had been set up, one at either end of the room; wine and beer only, no mixed drinks. I wondered briefly if anyone would hire my bartending service again.

Gwen surfaced from the crowd, wearing a black pants suit with a high-neck, long sleeve black blouse.

"Thank you for coming," she said, putting her hand lightly on my arm. Over Gwen's shoulder I spotted Stephen Morris, who greeted me with a raised eyebrow.

"Thank you for inviting me. You look nice."

"And you." She gave my arm a discrete squeeze before dropping her hand. Despite my best intentions, I caught myself recalling how she had touched me that night in my apartment.

"How did the judging go?" I asked as we strolled into the gallery.

"It was interesting, for the most part. A few heated moments, several close votes. Chris Stark did better than I expected, an honorable mention." She didn't say how Daniel fared and I didn't ask.

We passed a painting of a desert landscape dominated by a bleeding cross.

"What do you think of Montoya's crucifix?" she asked.

"Too emotional for my taste. But then, we Protestants are pretty much neck up when it comes to religious expression. A bookmark would be more appropriate."

Gwen drew back and looked at me as if I'd said something interesting. To cover my embarrassment I asked her what she wanted to drink, then headed across the room to the bar.

Stephen Morris caught up with me as I picked up two glasses of Chardonnay.

"Enjoying the opening?" he asked.

"So far. And you?"

"Always nice to see the work of our fine young artists. I never know when I'll find someone worth representing. Like your friend Daniel Lackland. Stunning piece. Have you seen it yet?"

"No, I just arrived."

"I know. I've been watching you. Quite friendly with the Widow Washburn."

"Actually I'm escorting her as a favor."

"I'm sure you are."

"I know her from the Longhorn," I added defensively. "She didn't want to come alone, so I volunteered."

"Of course you did. Any more news about our favorite Dallas gallery owner?"

"Not really," I said, trying to decide whether or not to tell Stephen about the poisoned scotch in the Longhorn. "How about you?"

"Not until now." He pointed across the gallery to where Gwen was talking with a fat man wearing a white suit and sporting a large mustache. Max Gregory. Gwen was stressing a point with her finger, almost jabbing Gregory in the chest. Gregory didn't yield.

"Excuse me," I said.

I threaded my way through the crowd, aware Gregory would recognize me. I didn't care. He'd threatened me, probably tried to kill me. I wasn't going to hide. And I wasn't going to let him torment Gwen.

"Here you are," I said, handing a glass to Gwen and maneuvering myself between her and Gregory.

Gregory looked up at me. I think he smiled under the curtain of hair hanging from his upper lip. Gwen put a hand on my shoulder as if to keep me from walking over Gregory.

She made a hurried introduction. "Max Gregory, Stu Carlson. Stu, if you could . . ."

"I do believe we've spoken before," said Gregory, ignoring Gwen and extending his moist hand. "I was just telling Mrs. Washburn here that I'm moving my little shop to Santa Fe. A much better location, don't you agree."

"Location isn't everything," I said.

"How true, my boy. There are times when one has nowhere to hide. It was a pleasure seeing you again. You, too, Mrs. Washburn."

He gave a slight bow and walked away. I turned toward Gwen.

"I don't need you to protect me," she said.

"I'm sure you don't." I held up my hands in surrender.

She stared at me for a few seconds, then smiled, the tension sliding from her face and neck.

"I'm sorry," she said. "I know you're trying to help. You were right. I found out Gregory had dealings with my husband, owed Andrew some money. I just want to be rid of him." She waved a hand toward the nearest set of paintings. "Let's talk about something else. Did you get a chance to see any more of the exhibition?"

We roamed the gallery, Gwen treating me to incisive commentary on the art and artists. She was generous to talent, merciless to pretenders. Two women, acquaintances of Gwen's, stopped us. As promised, she introduced me as the Reverend Carlson, an old friend.

While the women pressed Gwen for details of the judging, I wondered about Gregory. Had he said that he was moving to Santa Fe in order to admit defeat? Or was it yet another threat? I looked around the room. To my surprise, Gregory was talking to Stephen and another man I didn't recognize. Stephen seemed to be smiling; I couldn't tell if it was genuine.

Gwen snagged my arm again as a means of escape. We continued past a guillotine welded from used auto parts and ended up at the back of a small crowd. We waited our turn to get to the front. It was a small oil painting, not much bigger than a postcard. Daniel's painting, the landscape I had seen at the studio. A discrete card indicated Best of Show. The tiny canvas drew me into its sweeping distances. I glanced at Gwen.

"I refuse to believe he murdered Andrew," she said softly as she moved away from the painting. In a flash of jealous insight I realized nothing I would ever do or say could draw such a response from her.

We examined a wood carving of a pair of feet in wingtips, then stopped in front of Chris' painting. The background was dirty yellow mottled with grayer patches, like blooms of mold under old wallpaper. In the foreground, all in the lower third of the canvas, four rectangular blocks of black paint, as wide and rough as railroad ties, angled across one another. Below them, at the bottom of the canvas and resting on the horizontal, a single block of red.

"Does it remind you of anything?" I asked.

"Should it?"

I shrugged, not sure why I asked. Chris broke away from a group of people in the corner and joined us in front of his work.

"Madame Judge." He made a small bow.

"Hello, Chris. Congratulations."

"Yeah," I added. "Congratulations."

"What do you think, Stu?" He pointed to the painting with his beer bottle.

"I think it's a strong composition. I like it."

"It is that. Well, I'll leave you two alone. Thanks again for the ride." He wandered off in the direction of the nearest bar.

"You don't like him, do you?" I asked.

"Let's just say I have trouble with his type."

"What type is that?"

"Men who spend more time looking like artists than doing art."

"What do you think of the painting?"

"You really want to know?"

"Yes."

She moved us behind a large basket woven from bones and rusted metal bars, away from any listeners, before speaking.

"Technically he's proficient, but there isn't much life to his work. I'm not sure how to explain it. It's more craft than art. The paint is all placed just where it should be. That's the problem. He's the sort of painter who'd be best off as a minor figure in some school or movement, following the lead of some truly ground-breaking artists."

"You've got a great eye," I said, the words falling out before I realized the pun.

Gwen smiled graciously. "The only one I got." She looked across the crowd as if summing up. "I'm finished with my duties. Are you hungry yet?"

We finished our wine and headed for the exit. Near the entrance I caught our dressed-in-black reflection on the side of ten-foot, chrome-plated armadillo. We made a

Chapter ★ Twenty-Eight

handsome couple.

Outside, the world had changed. Towering, steel gray thunderheads, heavy as granite and ready to fall, filled the western sky. An elm tree across the parking lot flung its branches to the east, the pale green undersides of its leaves turning up in the steady wind.

Gwen climbed into her blue Mercedes. I followed in my pickup. Traffic lights danced on the end of their poles out over the intersection with Jarvis and the branches of oak trees in the park waved in procession like breakers tumbling onto a beach. Streetlights snapped on in the half-light.

I pulled into the driveway behind Gwen, rolled up the windows, and climbed out with the bottle of wine. We stood for a moment outside her door, enjoying the wind and the assurance of rain.

A cat I hadn't seen the other day, a Siamese with mad eyes and blue undercolor, greeted us at the door. I knelt down to make my acquaintance, letting the animal rub its head in my cupped palm.

"What's its name?" I asked.

"Marie Curie, because she glows in the dark. I call her Madame." Gwen touched my head lightly, then quickly moved away before I could stand up.

"I need to change before I start cooking," she said, going up the stairs across from the door.

"Take your time."

I hung my jacket on the bentwood coat tree, then inspected the living room—now fully coated in deep royal blue to match the dining room—through an archway. Heavy, Mission style furniture filled both rooms. A row of Hopi Kachinas danced on the wall above the sofa. A collection of watercolors, mostly hill country landscapes—some quite nice—covered the opposite wall. I looked closely. Signed Gwen Shepherd.

The table in the dining room was set for two—bone china, crystal, silver, the works. An armful of irises erupted from a cut-glass vase in the middle of the table.

The only work in the dining room was a small landscape of Daniel's over the weathered antique sideboard. I wondered if it hung there before the new paint job.

"I'll take that," said Gwen, sweeping the wine out of my hands and leading me into the kitchen, a bright room of polished pine and green Mexican tile. She wore blue jeans and a black, short sleeve shirt printed with a parrot whose blue tail feathers matched the walls. "Everything's almost ready. I just have to heat the bread, throw together the salad, and cook the linguine."

"Can I do anything?"

"You can sit there and keep me company."

I pulled out a chair from the table at the far end of the kitchen. Gwen's shoulders rose and fell under the thin fabric as she tossed the salad.

"Are you the Gwen Shepherd of the watercolors?" I asked.

"The height of my career as an artist. I did them the summer after college. Made me think I had talent. I leave them up to remind me what I'm not."

She set the salad bowl to one side and looked into a cabinet.

"Shit. I left the pine nuts in my car. Could you run out and get them? They're in a small paper bag from Delmonico's. The keys are in the basket by the door."

Drops of rain the size of grapes splattered on the brick walkway when I opened the front door.

"You got an umbrella?" I shouted.

"Try the closet."

I had to hold the small umbrella in front of me as a shield against the rain flying flat with the stiff wind. A strobe-like flash of lightning lit the underbelly of the clouds as I fumbled with the keys and lowered myself into the driver's seat of the Mercedes. I took a moment to admire the interior, then leaned over to pick up the bag of pine nuts from the floor of the passenger side. I touched the neck of a glass bottle. I pulled it out. Laphroig, four inches of whiskey remaining. The upper left corner of the label was scrunched above the red letter L.

I fingered the torn label. The wind died down as the heart of the storm opened up. Rain drummed on the roof and exploded off the windshield in a spray of liquid needles. It was the bottle from the Longhorn five days earlier.

Someone planted the bottle here to set her up, I rea-
soned, just the way Daniel was framed. The bottle was
stashed while she was asleep or at work or leaving the note
for me at the Longhorn. She couldn't have done it.

But she could have. Walter never saw her when she
stopped in the bar to leave me the note. She could have
switched the bottles then.

I shook myself, trying physically to clear a space
between trust and suspicion. I don't know that she tried to
poison me. All I have is the bottle. I should go back into
the townhouse and confront her. I owe her that much.

I restored the bottle to its hiding place and raced for
the townhouse under the meager shelter of the umbrella.
When I reentered the kitchen, Gwen was loading linguine
into boiling water.

"Have trouble finding the sack?"

"No, not at all." I put the small paper bag on the
counter. My brain stumbled for a way to bring up the
bottle in her car.

"I set the wine out on the table," she said. "Could you
open it?"

A two-handled corkscrew sat on the table next to the
Pinot Noir. I picked up the bottle. Just say it, I told myself
as I prepared to cut into the thin lead cover with the tip of
the screw.

"Gwen, while I was outside..."

I stopped. A hole the size of a pencil lead pierced the
burgundy colored sheath over the top of the bottle. It was
larger than the pin pricks that let the cork breathe and it
was located just over the inside lip of the glass beneath.

"What about outside?"

"The storm. It's really kicking up." I carefully cut away the lead cover, glancing up twice to make sure Gwen still had her back turned. The cork was seated lower than usual, a half inch down the neck of the bottle.

"Sounds like the clouds opened up," she agreed. "Feel free to put some music on. I picked up a Stevie Ray Vaughn CD yesterday. It's on the shelf in the living room."

"Great." I set the corkscrew and gently worked the cork upward, then poured a couple of ounces in a glass and lifted it to my nose. A faint smell of bitter almonds blended with grape and oak and cherry.

"Do you want some?" I offered.

"Sure. Just leave my glass on the table. Looks like good wine. Why don't you taste it and give me the expert opinion?"

I poured a second glass, then looked at Gwen. She stood at the counter with her back to me, mincing garlic with a ten-inch knife.

I pretended to swallow. "Mmm. It is good. Oh, I just forgot a surprise I have down in the truck." I was out the door, glass in hand, before she could reply.

Chapter ★ Twenty-Nine

Behind the driver's seat of my pickup I found an old coffee cup with a plastic lid. I rolled down the window and rinsed the cup in the rain. I transferred the wine to the cup, sealed on the cover, and stowed the cup in the glove compartment. I turned over the engine and backed into the street through a sheet of runoff trying to find its way to the river.

I pulled in at a Seven Eleven about a mile from Gwen's apartment and stared through the downpour at yellow and red sacks of potato chips inside the window. Beads of water trailed down the sides of my face and the wet fabric of my shirt clung to my chest. Maybe I was wrong. Maybe it was all a mistake. I pulled the coffee cup out of the glove compartment and gave myself another whiff. I have a good nose. No mistake. I had been out in Gwen's car for almost five minutes, enough time to slide a hypodermic needle in along the cork, suck out a few ounces of wine, and squirt in a concentrated solution of potassium cyanide.

I unknotted my bow tie and hung it over the rearview mirror as the threads of an ugly story wove together in my head. She had poisoned her husband's drink before leaving the reception. No doubt she had plenty of reasons. She hid a vial of cyanide at Daniel's studio and let him take the fall; her "soft spot" for Daniel was just an act. Then I made the mistake of telling her about Gregory. She was probably as deeply involved as her husband, maybe more. Something convinced her I was getting too close to the truth. Maybe she panicked when I showed up at the townhouse; maybe she knew I followed her to the lake house. So she brought me the note and swapped bottles of scotch after I conveniently mentioned I was the only one who drank from the single malts. She hadn't planned to poison me at her apartment. That was just a backup in case I failed to swallow the scotch she'd left at the Longhorn. I wasn't bothered that I couldn't figure out how she would explain a dead body at a dinner for two. Andrew's murder had been clever enough; I was sure she had a scheme for me.

I ducked into the store, got change for a dollar at the counter, and walked over to the pay phone mounted on the wall next to the soda cooler. The air-conditioning pulled goose bumps from my damp skin. I rang Ramirez's work number. Someone answered. I said it was urgent. I left my name and the phone number at my apartment and made them promise to track down the lieutenant.

I considered going back to the apartment and waiting for the phone to ring. I couldn't do it, not with the adrenaline from my escape still bouncing off the walls of my veins. I deposited a second quarter and tried Stephen

Morris' day number, then the night number. No answer. Who else? I'd already bothered Cheryl enough for one day. Rusty and Pauline and just about everyone else I trusted were at the Longhorn and I didn't want to fuel Brownie's silent anger by bringing the police there a second time. Maybe Chris. I called his apartment on the off chance he'd come home early. No answer, so I tried the studio. He picked up on the second ring.

"Chris, this is Stu. I think Gwen Washburn just tried to do it to me." A pair of skinny girls with braces pulled diet sodas out of the cooler and giggled. I glared and they scurried away.

"Do what?"

"Poison me." I cupped the mouthpiece with my hand. "Just a few minutes ago. In the wine, at her place."

"Did she say anything?"

"No. I saw the hole where she injected the cyanide and smelled it when I poured a glass. So I made up some excuse and ran out."

"Shit, Stu, that's bad. Did you call the police?"

"I already left a message for Ramirez to call me at my apartment."

"Where are you now?"

"At the Seven Eleven on Harris."

"Why don't you come over to the studio? I'll call back the police and have them call here."

"Thanks. I'll be there in five minutes."

The storm had settled into a warm, steady soak. The tires of the pickup sounded like a set of endless zippers on the wet pavement and sent up rooster tails of water at intersections where the storm sewers had backed up.

Outside the studio, the reflection of a blue-white security light on a warehouse on the opposite bank broke into a thousand pieces on the rain-spattered and swirling surface of the river. The water was already up at least four feet. The short run into the building left my head, shoulders, and the tops of my thighs soaked, again. I flicked a few drops out of my eyes. The new latch on the studio door hung open. I knocked. No one answered, so I pushed in.

"Chris?" The large room appeared deserted. The only light came from an old, shaded lamp on a worktable along the opposite wall. Rain beat on the dark panes of the large window panels above the table. I crossed the room and picked out a tube from the orderly rows of Daniel's paints. Chromium red. I unscrewed the cap and squeezed out a line on tabletop. It glistened in the circle of light like thick, fresh blood. Like the block of red in Chris' painting. That was when I remembered where I'd seen Chris' painting before. It was identical to a drawing in Daniel's notebook. I put down the tube and started searching through the supplies on the table.

Something cold and wet splashed on my back and legs. I spun around and a second wave doused my front. The smell of gasoline filled my head.

"Looking for something?" Chris asked. When I try to think back on how he looked that night, I don't find anything strange about him, no wild eyes or fiendish grin. He was just Chris, dressed in black and standing in the shadows with a twenty gallon gas can in his hands.

"What are you doing?" I stepped toward him.

He pulled a metal cigarette lighter out of his pocket, flipped open the top, and spun the thumb wheel. A small flame leapt from his hand. He adjusted a dial on the bottom of the lighter and the flame grew into a wavering knife blade.

"Chris, what's going on?" I moved back until I felt the worktable with my hands.

"I think you know." He knelt down and tipped over the metal canister. Gasoline pulsed out of the metal throat and spread in a widening pool on the floor. "You were looking for Daniel's notebooks."

"You poisoned Washburn, didn't you? But I can't figure out why." I knew that in Hollywood bad guys took time to explain their crimes. I hoped Chris had watched as many bad movies as I had.

"You were close to that," he said. "I followed you once to Dallas and twice to Tumble Lake. Remember that painting you found in the shed, the Bierstadt? I painted it, and more like it. I sell them to Washburn. Ten thousand a piece. Takes three months. I have a natural talent. Washburn approached me after I drew the dollar bill in art school. Begs me to do a painting. For three fucking years I'm painting this shit. He won't let go. Keeps pushing. Threatens to expose me if I didn't keep turning out fakes. You talked to people. The guy's a real bastard."

The last few ounces of gasoline dribbled out of the can onto the wood floor.

"You gave me the idea, Stu, saying somebody like Daniel could go over the edge. Bingo. I knew what to do." He knelt down and unscrewed the cap of a second twenty-gallon can without taking his eyes off me. A second tide of gasoline flowed across the floor. "You just did too good a job trying to help him. I was hoping you wouldn't get that far. You're a good bartender."

Events clicked in my head like tumbling dominoes. Chris framed Daniel for Washburn's murder. He tried to poison me with the scotch. He planted the scotch bottle in Gwen's car. He put the cyanide in the wine. The wine I had left on the table for Gwen.

"Chris, this is between you and me. Let me call Gwen. I'll tell her I put cyanide in the bottle."

"I can't do that." He backed slowly toward the door. "She's in the way. You and she are supposed to make a toast and die in each other's arms. Then I go over and put the cyanide and syringe in her car and we got a lovers' suicide and murder."

I watched the flame bob and weave in the darkness. Gasoline fumes burned in my nose. The dark stain on the floor reached my feet.

"What about the people in this building? Are they just in the way, too?"

"There's no one here tonight. I've already checked." He groped around behind him for the handle on the door.

"And what about Daniel? What did he ever do?"

Chris froze at the mention of Daniel. "It was the only way. Somebody had to take the blame for Washburn's murder."

"Are you sure it isn't because Daniel's a real artist and you're not?"

"No." He slammed his fist against the metal door. I glanced quickly over my shoulder at the windows above the table. The panels didn't seem to be latched. I slid my hand along the table toward the lamp.

"I think you couldn't stand seeing Daniel create real art while you painted imitations. You were jealous and you wanted him out of the way."

"No. That's not true!"

"I think you did this whole thing so you could steal his ideas. Like that painting in the exhibition, the one you borrowed from his notebook. You just want to copy his work and take credit for it yourself."

"No! I'm an artist! A fucking artist!"

My fingers closed around the base of the lamp. I pulled hard and flung the lamp toward the door in a single motion. The room filled with blackness. I jumped onto the worktable and hurled myself at the dim outline of the window panel. The metal frame swung open and I was in the air. Night turned to day and a wall of fire slammed me into the river.

The water hit my side like a dozen baseball bats, knocking the air out of my lungs. The dark river closed in and its angry currents pulled me down, fighting for possession of my arms and legs. My arm snagged on a submerged branch. I grabbed hold and pushed my face toward the surface. A breath that was half air, half water filled my burning lungs. I was ten feet from the tumbled slope of the bank. Two hundred feet upstream and fifteen feet above the river, the open window coughed balls of orange flame that shuddered in the heavy rain and disappeared. I let go of the branch and the river swept me another hundred feet before I could fight my way to the edge.

I crawled out over chunks of broken concrete to reach a gravel path that ran between the river and the fence of the school bus parking lot. Through the chain links I spotted my truck parked outside the building. A section of the front wall exploded into the street, engulfing the pickup in a torrent of fire and bricks. I followed the fence in the other direction.

I ran down the middle of a deserted street of warehouses and businesses, the sound of my steps drowned out by the steady hammering of rain on pavement and walls. A sharp pain cut into my side with each step, as if I was being jabbed with a broken broom handle. I found a phone booth outside a dry cleaners. I slid my last coins in the slot and punched Gwen's number. Dear God, Gwen, pick up the phone. It rang ten times before I dropped the receiver. I started running. The blocks of businesses, apartment buildings, and bungalows dissolved together until the world held only three things: the rise and fall of my feet, the stabbing in my side, and the words of petition. Please God, let her live, I'll preach, I'll do anything, let her live. Somewhere behind me sirens screamed.

I saw the row of townhouses from two blocks away. A car pulled out and slowed as it went past me. It wasn't the blue Mercedes.

Gwen's door was slightly ajar. The high pitched wail of a smoke detector was clearly audible from the front walk. The door of the next townhouse opened.

"911," I shouted. The face blinked at me. "An ambulance. Get a fucking ambulance."

I pushed back Gwen's door. A thick, gray haze, carrying the sharp tang of burnt food and plastic, covered the ceiling of the living room and dining room. I ran to the kitchen. Smoke rose in a column from a saucepan that glowed red on the bottom. A shattered wineglass lay on the floor in a circle of red wine. Somewhere overhead the alarm gave its useless warning.

"Gwen! Gwen!" No answer.

I rushed back to the living room and was about to climb the stairs when I noticed a sandaled foot poking out from a door near the entrance.

Gwen lay on her side in front of the toilet in the small bathroom, her knees drawn up to her chest. I dropped to the floor beside her. Her cheek rested in a pool of vomit. As I lifted her head a spasm shook her body and she coughed up more thin, bitter liquid. Her breathing was shallow but steady.

"You'll be okay, Gwen," I said, pulling her into my lap. "Everything's going to be fine."

Vehicles and voices assembled in the street.

Chapter ★ Thirty

When I was six years old I asked God to give me wings. Every night, for months, the same request, "Let me fly." Nothing ever happened; I never soared or swooped or amazed the world. I know now that prayer doesn't work that way, if it works at all. But sometimes, when the world's tumbling down and the thing most needed and desired suddenly appears, it sure feels that way.

I sat in the back of a patrol car, huddled in the wet sheep and hay smell of a police blanket, as they wheeled Gwen out to the ambulance. An IV was hooked to her arm, oxygen mask over her mouth. The yellow-white flicker of the gas lamps by the door glinted off the wet surface of the plastic sheet that protected her from the drizzle. Her eyes were still closed, only now more as if she were asleep than unconscious. The attendants, their heads bowed against the light rain, rolled the stretcher into the open back of the white and blue van. The red taillights flared, then subsided to a steady glow as the ambulance pulled away from the curb. Madame the cat peered down from an upstairs window.

A scrap of liturgy rolled through my head. "It is right, and a good and joyful thing, always and everywhere to give thanks to you, Father Almighty, Creator of heaven and earth."

On the way to the Med Center an icy numbness crept over me. I knew my ribs hurt, but I didn't mind the pain, as if someone had unplugged the wires to my body. And I was shivering, although I didn't feel cold. The rain had stopped. The branches of the trees along the streets sagged low and exhausted, black against the dark sky. At an intersection, a row of cars waited in line for a chance to ford a small lake that came up to the bottom of the doors. Small waves spread out behind the passing vehicles like the flow of gasoline across the floor of the studio. I wondered if the rain had put out the fire.

At the hospital, Drainer dogged me from the examining room, to the x-ray room, then back to the examining room to have two cracked ribs taped up. One of the residents, who recognized me as a friend of Cheryl's, found me a scrub suit to wear in place of my soaked clothes. Someone said Gwen was going to be okay. They gave me codeine for the pain, warned me to watch for coughed-up blood, and released me to Drainer's care.

I spent the rest of the night in a small, green room at police headquarters, going over my story with Ramirez and Drainer. I'd given them a quick version when they first arrived at Gwen's apartment. Now Ramirez took me through it slowly. The codeine had kicked in; I recounted the events as if describing a movie of someone else's life.

They left twice, once to search Chris' apartment, the second time to search his car, parked two blocks from the studio. In the apartment they found a second studio, with enlarged photographs of the Bierstadt and a "Russell" in progress. Inside the car they discovered a vial of cyanide and a large syringe stashed in Chris' black bag. They waited until the next day to pick through the burned-out shell of the old Texas Sun factory. Enough of Chris' body remained for identification. You could probably say the same for my truck. By six a.m. Ramirez accepted my story, although I didn't tell him about the lake house. A patrol car drove me home.

My feet were blocks of concrete on the steps. The sun was beginning to show over the rooftops and the air felt cool and light, with a hint of moisture. Inside the apartment I fell onto the bed. The painkiller was wearing off, but I didn't have the energy to take another pill. I couldn't remember when I'd eaten.

Rusty and Cheryl woke me at two in the afternoon to bring me lunch and loan me Rusty's road car, a '78 Lincoln Continental. The hospital grapevine had given Cheryl a rough outline of my night and I filled in some details over chicken-fried steak from Mac's. I promised Cheryl not to lift anything heavier than a beer bottle and to show up for an exam on Monday.

Alone again in my kitchen, I brewed a pot of coffee and drank it black. Despite a rib that ached like a broken fence post, I held off on the codeine. I called the hospital. Yes, Gwen Washburn was awake. Yes, she was receiving visitors. I arrived twenty minutes later, expecting to find family members or one of the friends I'd met at the opening. Not Daniel.

The curtains in the private room were closed, the only light a small reading lamp by the bed, which was raised to a sitting position. Gwen, her face pale and an IV still tied to her arm, appeared tired and frail, her hair spread out on the pillow.

"Stu," said Daniel, leaping to his feet when I leaned my head into the room. Like a child at Christmas, I thought. He had a pad and pencil in his hand. "Come in. Come in. Have a seat."

He ushered me into the chair by the bed. I glanced at Gwen. She was smiling, weakly, at Daniel, who had gone around to stand on the other side of the bed.

"The police let me out," he said, his words tripping over one another. "Of jail. This morning. They said you had something to do with it. I knew it. I knew you'd help me. Thank you. My mother says thank you, too. She just left."

"Daniel," said Gwen, touching his hand. "Could I speak to Stu alone for a minute?"

"Sure, Gwen. I'll try to reach your brother again. Stu, I have something. For you. I'll bring it to the bar. Tomorrow."

Daniel set the pad and pencil on the bed, then left. A moment later he stuck his head back in the door.

"And thank you," he said. "For saving Gwen." Then he was gone.

"He likes to take care of me," she said, staring at the door. Her voice was raspy and small, as if someone had sandpapered the inside of her throat. "Of course, I do most of the taking care."

She finally looked at me.

"Reverend," she said, lifting her hand, then letting it drop to the sheet. "I'm afraid I don't have much energy. I don't know if it's the drugs or the after-effects of the cyanide."

"I'm glad you're recovering."

"Thank you. The doctor says I may have an ulcer, but no other permanent damage."

We both looked at the pad of paper, a partial sketch of Gwen's face that conveyed both beauty and infirmity.

"That's right," she said, almost a whisper. "Daniel needs me. I need him." She paused for a moment to gather her strength. "The police told me what happened. You found me in the bathroom. Sent for the ambulance. But you were at the studio. Something about a fire. I don't understand." She struggled to keep her eyes open. I looked down at my hands and delivered the speech I'd rehearsed on the way to the hospital.

"Chris tried to poison me at the bar on Friday night. Only at the time I didn't know who did it. He left the evidence in your car and I found it when I went for the pine nuts. So I came back in, ready to ask you about it. Then I saw that the wine had been tampered with. I thought it was you. I was wrong and you paid for it. I'm sorry. I poured the wine, pretended to take drink, then ran. Leaving you with a poisoned glass. All because of me. Chris wanted to get me and you were just in the way."

I looked up. She had fallen asleep. I don't know how much she heard. I pressed the button to lower the bed, turned out the lamp, and let myself out of the room.

On the elevator, fatigue swept over me like a warm,

swelling wave on the beach at Galveston. If it hadn't been for a sharp volley of pain from my busted ribs, I might have curled up in a chair in the lobby. In my fog I nearly collided with someone outside the hospital gift shop.

I recoiled as the slight jarring sent fresh stabbing into my side. It was all I could do not to scream at the person who crossed my path. I stepped back.

The woman had short, black hair, nicely cut, and a blue suit, the outfit of a lawyer or a corporate vice-president. Except for the face. Green eyes on the verge of sadness. Thick black eyebrows. Full lips and round cheeks.

Jocelyn. I could hear her voice almost before she spoke.

"Stuart. What a surprise." She reached to hug me. I backed away.

"Please. Don't. Broken ribs."

"I'm so sorry. Did I hurt you? Here, let me help you sit down."

I pulled my arm out of her hand. A week earlier I would have exploded, told her to leave me alone, leave my town, my life. But not now. I stepped back to look at her. Her earrings, gold loops, matched her styled hair and tailored clothes. When we were married, Jocelyn always wore intense clothes—shawls, sandals, ponchos, scarves, peasant dresses—adorned with items of moral or political significance; a cloth ribbon from the rain forest, a necklace crafted in the South African townships. She looked like a different person. I felt like one.

"I'm fine, Jocelyn."

"Good, good. I was worried about you, Stuart, not returning my messages. I was afraid you were depressed or angry. I so want us to forgive one another and reestablish our friendship. I really believe we can grow through healing."

For the first time in the eight years I'd known her, I felt no need to misbehave or argue or compete. I didn't want anything from her and I didn't have anything I wanted to give.

"I think not," I said. "You know where I work. Stop in sometime and I'll buy you a beer." I turned and walked away.

Chapter ⋆ Thirty-One

Daniel stopped in the Longhorn on Monday to give me a present. Not the actual thing—the painting's due to hang in the ArtFest exhibition for another two months—but to tell me he wanted me to have it. I'll hang it behind the bar. It's too good to sit alone in a small apartment over a hardware store.

Stephen Morris called to say Gregory had definitely moved. I doubt the police will follow up on vague suggestions of counterfeit art dealing. Case closed. I'll probably never find out how much Gwen really knew and I don't care. As Harry would say, "The answer, my friend, is blowing in the wind."

Tuesday morning the insurance company informed me I'd get a thousand dollars for my truck, twelve hundred tops. That night I bought a scotch-and-soda for John Springer and told him I'd preach in August. I'm no closer to faith than when he first asked. Maybe I'll be one of those lucky ones who bumps into it again.